The memories [...]
seemed to com [...]
instead of ten years ago.

Leigh had known even then that there would never be anyone for her but Jake Ryker. He'd been exciting, with his dark, brooding looks, his unpredictability. He'd awakened something wonderful and unfamiliar within her whenever he fixed those blue eyes of his on her.

And she'd been certain he didn't know she was alive. But a chance meeting at the lake had changed everything.

He'd kissed her.

And kissed her. Stolen kisses on a rainy evening had changed her forever. She'd been aware of nothing but the heat of his mouth, the warmth of his caresses.

Jake Ryker had been her first love, the one she gave up her innocence to. He'd taught her about passion, about heat. He'd made her yearn.

And most of all, he'd made her weep...

Jake Ryker's Back in Town

JENNIFER MIKELS

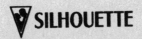

SILHOUETTE

SPECIAL EDITION

First published in Great Britain in 1995
by Silhouette Books, Eton House, 18-24 Paradise Road,
Richmond, Surrey TW9 1SR

© Suzanne Kuhlin 1994

Silhouette, Silhouette Special Edition and Colophon are
Trade Marks of Harlequin Enterprises B.V.

ISBN 0 373 09929 0

23-9505

Made and printed in Great Britain

JENNIFER MIKELS

started out an avid fan of historical novels, which eventually led her to contemporary romances, which in turn led her to try penning her own novels. She quickly found she preferred romantic fiction with its happy endings to the technical writing she'd done for a public relations firm. Between writing and raising two boys, the Phoenix-based author has little time left for hobbies, though she does enjoy cross-country skiing and antique shopping with her husband.

Other Silhouette Books by Jennifer Mikels

Silhouette Special Edition

A Sporting Affair
Whirlwind
Remember the Daffodils
Stargazer
Double Identity
Freedom's Just Another Word
A Real Charmer
A Job for Jack
Your Child, My Child
Denver's Lady

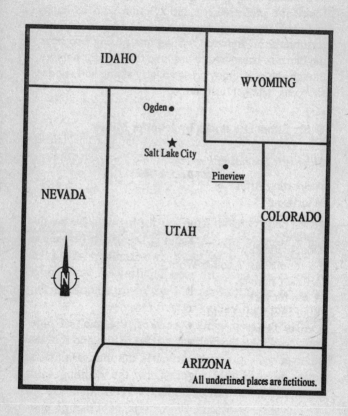

IDAHO

WYOMING

Ogden ●

★
Salt Lake City

● Pineview

NEVADA

COLORADO

UTAH

N

ARIZONA

All underlined places are fictitious.

Chapter One

Rain pelted the car window, dueling with the swishing windshield wipers. The dim headlights beamed a narrow tunnel on the dark, two-lane highway. Jake Ryker could have driven it blindfolded. As if he'd never been away, he recalled every twist and turn in the mountain road leading toward Pineview.

With the Jeep window cracked, the smell of pine trees bordering the highway wafted to him and the late summer's air promised an early autumn. He'd left town on a similar night. Only the droning rain pounding at the roof of his Jeep was different now.

Ten years, he mused. Before this, he'd had no reason to leave Salt Lake City and return to the small Utah town. He'd thought time healed everything and wondered now if that were true. Softly he cursed. He was eight miles from town, and Leigh McCall's image was like a haunting apparition on the road before him.

Memories flashed in his mind, more bad than good. There'd been only one worth remembering. But the boy who'd yearned for one girl was gone. And the girl, a woman now, married, was a fragment of his past.

Instinctively he braked as he came to the final turn before town, a hairpin curve that vowed danger to the less observant. During the day, tourists traveled it with mindless caution, too enraptured by the breathtaking views and ascending, pine-dotted mountains. Locals understood the road's menace, and when slick with rain, it taunted even the prudent driver.

Jake maneuvered around the first curve of the S, but as he began the second, he caught a glimpse of flares. He squinted through the curtain of rain at the flashing red light atop a sheriff department's cruiser and the ambulance blocking the road ahead of him.

Headlights sliced a projection of light on the opposite side of the highway and the sports car with its rear end squashed like an accordion, its nose dipped toward the incline.

Jake edged onto the shoulder of the road behind the deputy's car. Pushing open his door, he was met by a cacophony of sound—wind whistling through stirring pines and aspens, voices murmuring from shadowy figures, steam hissing in the night air and funneling up from a damaged radiator.

Hunching his shoulders against the rain, he raised the collar of his Windbreaker while noting that the other car's left front end had been ripped away. Be-

neath the blurry mantle of the rainy night, three people in rain gear huddled over someone at the back of
the ambulance. If things hadn't changed in town, they
were Doc Higley, the driver and a volunteer. Town
services relied on volunteers. But then, ten years had
passed and that might have changed.

His feet slipping beneath him, he descended the
muddy incline toward the deputy. "Need help?"

The beam of a flashlight blasted against Jake's eyes.
"He's conscious but stuck in here," the deputy yelled
over the wail of the wind, then flashed the light back
inside the car. "Think he has a leg injury."

"I'll try to get in from the other side." Jake plod-
ded only three steps through the mud at the back of
the sports car. The deputy was murmuring assurances
to the driver, and a voice was calling out from across
the highway, but sounds faded as another sense took
over. Jake sniffed hard as if needing confirmation that
the smell of gasoline was permeating the air.

He scurried back to the deputy and snatched the
crowbar from his hand. "We have to get him out.
Now," he insisted, bending forward inside the car. He
wiggled a hand down. Blindly he groped in the narrow space between the metal and the driver's foot and
winced when metal snagged his palm.

"It hurts," the driver mumbled.

Jake blocked his own pain and made quick eye
contact with him. "It's going to hurt more in a moment. Okay?"

The man managed a nod and grimaced as Jake
wedged in the crowbar and leaned into it until he heard

the metal snap. The man's cry echoed over the keening wind as they tugged him from the car, and Jake hoisted him over his shoulder. It ached from another wound, still healing. Mud sucking at his feet, he labored up the incline and trailed the deputy across the road. In the distance, the high wail of a siren floated on the air.

As he eased the man to the pavement, a figure in a yellow slicker hovered near, then knelt down. "Everything will be fine," a feminine voice assured the driver.

Wind masked the voice, but Jake would have known it anywhere. Through the blinding rain, he stared at the face that had intruded into too many of his dreams for too many years.

Behind them, a fire engine roared to a stop on the highway. Two more men rushed forward to lift the man inside the ambulance.

Straightening, she turned with a smile toward him. "Thank you for..." She paused, her smile fading. "Jake?"

Rain plastered back strands of hair peeking out from the hood of her slicker. The glow of a flare bathed her delicate features. And for a heartbeat, her eyes locked with his. Jake slipped a hand under her arm and tugged her to a stand. "It's been a long time."

In the manner of someone trying to see more clearly, she wiped a hand across her wet face. "You're—"

"Back," he finished for her.

From the ambulance, someone called to her.

She broke the stare and stole a glance over her shoulder. "I have to go."

He wanted to keep her near a moment longer, but she'd already swung away and was scrambling into the ambulance. Yanking a handkerchief from his jeans pocket, Jake pressed it to his palm to ease the throbbing and wrapped the cloth around his bloody hand. Beside him, the deputy said something. He didn't answer.

In the midst of bedlam and hoses snaked across the highway, all he saw was her. Even after the ambulance doors closed, he didn't move. He'd never expected this, he realized. Ten years ago, he'd loved the one girl in town he should never have even looked at. During minutes on a rainy dark night, he wondered if that changed.

The funeral for his father had taken place two weeks ago. Jake had expected nothing; that was what he'd gotten.

Inside Henry Linser's office, morning sunlight streamed through the blinds while Linser bluntly told him, "All your father had was the house."

A two-room cottage that Jake had called home for too many years.

In a trained, polite voice, the town's lawyer and Realtor offered a condolence, then went on without taking a breath. "Details were handled, but there are funeral expenses. Now, the bank would be willing to buy the house."

Jake wondered if Linser thought he'd fallen off a turnip truck. "Since the house isn't worth much, I gather the land is valuable."

"It's land," Henry said in a matter-of-fact tone. "The town's growing. Any land becomes valuable when in demand. They'll give you a fair price for it."

"Handle it."

Seeming pleased at Jake's agreeableness, Henry nodded. "I didn't think you'd want to keep it."

In truth, Jake was glad to get rid of it. That shack across the railroad tracks harbored too many memories that he wanted to lose.

"You might want to check it out. I don't know what your father had, but some of your own belongings might still be there."

"I'll do it later."

"Good." Henry settled back, relaxing in his wing-armed chair. "I'll handle the business side of this as quickly as possible. I imagine you'll want to leave soon."

Jake raised his eyes to him. "Why would you think that?"

The lawyer shifted on his chair and rubbed a spot between his brows. "Well, you didn't come back for the funeral, so I thought—well, everyone thought—you might be too busy."

Busy in a hospital bed, recovering from a bullet wound in the shoulder. If he'd been able to make the funeral, he'd have come. His father was the only family he'd ever had, though Jake couldn't honestly remember a genuine family moment between them.

"The town's changed—sort of."

Jake wasn't interested in small talk but remained seated. He'd give Henry a passing grade for politeness.

Swiveling his chair away from the desk, Henry peered through the blinds at the street. "Clyde Banner still gets drunk every Friday and Saturday night," he said.

Clyde, a short, ruddy-faced man, had always haunted the local bars in the evening. But unlike Jake's father, who'd been passed out most mornings, Clyde had always managed to meet Lester Newell at eight in the morning at Bensen's Garage for a game of checkers. "Does he still play checkers every morning with Lester?"

"Still does. And Clyde's as nosy as ever," Henry gibed. "But he isn't as nosy as Lester's wife. Grace will always win that award hands down. So I guess people haven't changed."

No, he hadn't thought they would have. It was one of the reasons why he'd never come back. He wondered if Henry was trying to offer a subtle warning that he wasn't any more welcome now than he used to be.

"And Abby Martin still runs this town."

Jake doubted Abigail Martin had ever favored being called by such a common nickname as Abby. But, like Henry, a lot of people in Pineview grew up with her. She could live on the hill in a house with twenty rooms, but Leigh's aunt would always be Abby to them.

"People are talking. You're a real hero around here after last night." As friendly as Henry had been, Jake didn't miss the hint of amazement in his voice.

"I saw Leigh McCall at the accident."

Henry's round cheeks bunched with a broader grin. "She'd be there if someone needed help. Lovely as ever."

"Why was she there?"

"She's got one of those scanners over at the diner."

"She's still working at the diner?" Six months after he'd left town, he'd called his father and learned she'd married. He'd assumed her aunt had found her a respectable match, someone who'd sweep her up to one of the huge Victorians on the hill.

"As always, the deputies hang out there, so she always knows what's going on. She started helping her uncle again after her husband died." Henry squinted as if visualizing a time past. "It happened only a year after you left, I think. She's had some hard times," he added.

A widow. It was news he'd never expected. He wanted to ask more, but as Henry checked the digital clock on his desk, Jake took his cue and stood.

"So will you be leaving soon?"

Jake imagined most people would ask the same question. He halted at the door and met Henry's stare with a steely one. "I haven't made plans." He hadn't anticipated a welcome party. People were slow to forgive or forget in a small town, but he'd thought they'd give him some benefit of doubt. "When I'm ready," he answered before closing the door behind him and heading toward his car.

Though it was Saturday morning, the quiet was marred by a few people shuffling along the sidewalk or the occasional pickup truck driving by. At the barbershop, a teenager was sweeping off the sidewalk, and two doors away, the owner of a dress shop was changing a mannequin in the display window.

Henry was right. Little had changed. Unconsciously Jake gripped the steering wheel tighter and felt pain in his palm beneath the makeshift bandage.

Wondering if Doc Higley's office was still across the street from McCall's Diner, he wheeled onto Pineview's picture-perfect Main Street, with its old lampposts and cobblestone sidewalks. A cool, early-morning breeze fluttered the leaves of trees and a banner stretched across the main street announced the upcoming Founder's Day celebration. Tourism was the town's livelihood. Without the fishermen or hunters or campers who traipsed to the woods for weekend getaways, Pineview would have been a ghost town centuries ago. The two big events in town had always focused on the Founder's Day Rodeo and the Independence Day celebration.

In the distance, Jake could see the slanted roof of the high school and the drive-in's arched sign. During his senior year, he'd hung out at that drive-in almost every night, because Leigh would be there. God, he'd been crazy about her, and because of her, he'd begun to change. She'd drawn out a gentleness in him that he hadn't known existed. She'd soothed his anger and tamed his rebelliousness, and he'd started to think about the future. All of that had ended one June night, but even after he'd left, he'd vowed to come back for her. Only within a month, she'd sought another, as if everything they'd shared had never happened.

It was over, he reminded himself. A person was allowed to be a fool in his youth.

The morning was slow at the diner. Leigh almost wished for more to keep her busy, but only a few regulars had wandered in. Near the cook's counter, she swiped butter across Clyde Banner's toast.

Beside her, her sister Kathleen sliced a cantaloupe. "He's back, isn't he?"

Leigh didn't look up. "Who told you?"

"Everyone is talking about him. Talk is he was a hero last night."

Leigh found such gossip ironic. Few people would have said a good word about Jake ten years ago. "Fickle group, aren't they? Until last night, everyone thought he'd be in jail by now."

"You didn't," Kathleen reminded her. "I didn't."

Leigh dropped to her haunches and reached into a cabinet for jelly packets. Years ago, Jake had been an angry young man. She'd always thought it was justified anger. People hadn't treated him fairly, especially her family.

"Hand me the pineapple," Kathleen requested as Leigh stood. "I never understood why Dad didn't like him." A faint frown shadowed her sister's face. "On second thought, I guess I know why. He was a hellion by Pineview's standards, always in some fight,'' she rambled on while adding diced pineapple to the cantaloupe chunks.

''He wasn't the one who started them,'' Leigh said in his defense.

There'd always been too many taunts about him being a bastard, about his drunk of a father being forced into a shotgun marriage. Then, later, she'd listened to the accusations leveled against Leonard Ryker and had known each one must have cut into Jake, too. She'd agonized with him, each slur against him slashing her because she'd felt as one with him.

More memories kept returning. They seemed to come from yesterday, instead of ten years ago. She'd known at fifteen that there would never be another for her. He'd been the boy all the girls talked about, only dreamed about because they were wary of him. For a while, she'd dutifully listened to her father's command to stay away from the Ryker boy. But secretly she'd watched him.

He'd been exciting with his dark, brooding looks, his unpredictability. He'd been the only boy in town to own a motorcycle, the only boy who'd awakened something wonderful and unfamiliar within her whenever he'd fixed those blue eyes on her. A rebel— defiant and confident at an age when most boys were floundering to understand themselves—he'd been the only boy her father would never have accepted.

At school, she'd snatched glances at him, certain he didn't know she was alive. Then one rainy afternoon, a chance meeting at the lake changed everything. Sweet sixteen. She'd been used to boys, as innocent and inexperienced as she was, who'd delivered chaste kisses under the porch light.

She'd left in the middle of Candy St. James's sixteenth birthday party and had strolled to the lake and found Jake sitting on a boulder.

He'd kissed her.

And kissed her. Stolen kisses on a rainy evening had changed her forever. She'd been aware of nothing but the heat of his mouth, the warmth from his caresses.

And she'd been scared, knowing she'd been close to lying in the wet grass with him, with Jake Ryker, the boy she'd been told to stay away from.

The warnings from her family hadn't mattered. To be with him, she'd defied her father and aunt, certain they were wrong about Jake. He'd been her first love, the one she'd given up her innocence to. He'd also been her only love. He'd taught her about passion, about heat. He'd made her yearn.

Most of all, he'd made her weep....

"Wake up," Kathleen teased, squeezing between Leigh and the counter.

For the first time that morning, Leigh met her sister's eyes and saw the happiness sparkling in them. God, but Kathleen deserved some. Too much sadness had touched her sister's life, too. "Is something wonderful going on?"

Kathleen smiled. "I've been trying not to tell anyone because there's nothing really to tell yet. But he hinted last night."

The *he* was Jim Baylor. For ten months, he'd been romancing Kathleen in Hollywood fashion—making her romantic dinners, sending flowers, taking her dancing. "Did he ask or just hint?"

"Hint."

"You're right," Leigh teasingly agreed. "That doesn't mean anything."

"Why do you think I'm upset? If he'd asked, I'd just be a nervous wreck."

Leigh laughed, happy her sister had found someone again. "He'll ask. And you'll say yes. Why are you acting so crazy?"

"Because he hasn't asked yet." A little dreamy eyed, Kathleen lounged against the counter. "Best of all, the kids love Jim. Before they get back from camp, I'd like to have this settled."

"So ask him to marry you."

"I can't do that."

"Why not?"

"It's not romantic."

Shrugging, Leigh pivoted away. Despite everything Kathleen had gone through, she still believed in the happily-ever-after myth. Leigh had abandoned the notion ten years ago.

Banishing more memories, she brought forward a smile and served the postal carrier his eggs and bacon. While filling a sugar container, she watched Kathleen. Head bent, a rag in her hand, she circled one spot on the restaurant counter, even though it was sparkling clean.

As Leigh rounded the counter and crossed to the table by the wall of windows to collect dirty dishes, the bell above the door rang. Her sister beamed at the man who came in. Lean and tall, Jim Baylor wouldn't win any best-looking award, but he was solid and stable, and sensitive to Kathleen's problems. He was exactly the kind of man she needed after her louse of a husband had abandoned her and the two kids without a backward look.

"A pretty thing like you shouldn't be working here," an elderly man at an adjacent table said, grinning at Leigh.

She responded to the mischief in his eyes. "And you'd take me away from all this, right?"

"Sure wouldn't mind."

"He said the same thing to me yesterday," Kathleen quipped, breezing by.

The man's weathered face wrinkled more. "Shoot! You weren't supposed to tell her that."

Leigh laughed and scooted past a table of regulars who worked at a nearby construction company. Spotting Lester and Grace Newell at a window table, she brought her cheeriest smile forward. "Morning, Lester. Grace." They reminded Leigh of the Jack Sprat nursery rhyme. Reed thin, his Adam's apple bobbing when he talked, Lester disappeared in his wife's shadow. Though he came in often, his wife preferred the country-club restaurant. "Coffee for both of you?"

"That would be fine, Leigh." Lester fiddled with a spoon. "And one of your doughnuts."

"Be right back with the doughnut." She bused a table, stacking plates. "Want the powdered sugar or the chocolate?"

"You know my sweet tooth."

"Chocolate, it is."

"Did you hear?" Grace asked insistently, stopping Leigh from stepping away. "Jake Ryker is back." Leigh didn't doubt Grace had already hightailed over to Aunt Abby's this morning to deliver that news. The woman pursed her lips. "I never thought he'd come back." Why she had joined her husband at the diner this morning became obvious. The gossip wasn't half as interesting at the country club.

"I guess you thought wrong," Leigh said.

As a bridge buddy of Grace's came in, she was sidetracked, expounding to her friend about the wonderful food she'd had at a neighboring town's Elks Club during a wedding reception for her niece.

When Leigh returned with their order, she received Grace's full attention again. "I told Kathleen that I'd recommend the Elks Club for her wedding reception."

Leigh poured her coffee. "Do you know something Kathleen doesn't? I didn't know she'd been asked yet?"

"Oh, I thought she had."

Though Leigh disliked the woman's gossipy nature, she admired her clever techniques for obtaining gossip.

"What about you, Leigh?" Her voice oozed with saccharin sweetness. "When are you going to go down the aisle again? The bank's new assistant manager seems sweet on you.''

"We're friends." As a bus-tour crowd started wandering in, Leigh joined Kathleen at the counter.

Kathleen retrieved a can of maple syrup from a cupboard. "Is Grace in top form?"

"She's ready to offer you wedding advice."

Kathleen moaned.

"Me, too."

"According to Grace, who are you in the throes of passion with?" Kathleen asked, sounding amused.

Leigh twisted the lid of a salsa jar. "Mark."

Kathleen concentrated on pouring maple syrup into a large white pitcher. "Maybe you should listen to her."

"Bite your tongue." Marriage to Mark Wendley had never entered her mind.

Frowning, Kathleen concentrated on the thick, sticky liquid plopping into the pitcher. "He likes you a lot."

"And I like him." But not enough. Once already, she'd married out of need more than want. Never again. Though she'd cared about her husband, the love with Ken had paled in comparison to what she'd felt for Jake. Ken had been more her father's choice than her own. Still, she'd suffered, stunned and shocked by loss when he'd died. She hadn't been prepared for it. Time had helped her recover from it, but she wasn't sure she ever wanted to take such a risk again.

"No, I mean he *really* likes you," Kathleen said, cutting into Leigh's thoughts.

Leigh grimaced as she placed more pressure on the lid. "What do you want me to do? I don't feel the same way about him." She felt no thrill, no need to learn any of his likes or dislikes. She felt no fire.

"Try harder," her sister suggested. "Visualize people describing you twenty years from now. You'll be called the Widow Grentham."

"I could be called worse things."

"You're impossible."

"No, you're in love. So you can't imagine anyone not wanting to be as euphoric as you are."

"He'd give you what you want. He has a nice, safe job at the bank."

Leigh pulled a face. "Mark isn't the one."

"I was afraid you were going to say that. Who is?"

"I'll know him when he walks through that door."

"You're fighting—" Kathleen looked past her as the bell above the café door tinkled.

A stillness settled over the diner, as the buzz of voices and clanging of silverware ceased. Frowning, Leigh angled a look over her shoulder.

In a slow movement, Jake Ryker slid mirrored sunglasses down to perch on his nose, then gave her a familiar slow smile, one that used to weaken her knees.

His thick dark hair was wind tossed, framing a face of sharp angles. Deep-set blue eyes smiled at her. She'd often thought they mirrored his moods, their piercing quality equally threatening and sensual. She found herself staring at his mouth, at his full bottom lip, and remembering. "Jake."

"In the flesh."

Chapter Two

Two men on stools at the counter frowned at him, a usual reaction from the locals toward a stranger, and he was one now. Peripherally he saw Grace Newell leaning toward her friends at another table, yet he ignored them all. From a jukebox, Reba McEntire tugged at heartstrings as she wailed out a soulful tale about a lover who'd broken her heart. Jake felt caught in a time warp. Ten years ago, he'd stood in the same spot, staring at the same woman and aching for her.

Last night he'd caught only a glimpse of her. Now, her hair, flaming in the glow of sunlight, was pulled back and held away from her face. The strands shone like copper. Dark eyes that rivaled the richness of the night sky remained locked with his.

Fragile. It was the only word to describe her. He soaked his mind with the image of her face—a romantic, delicate face with fine bones and a pouting mouth.

He'd never intended to get involved with her, but unknowingly, with a smile one afternoon after a football game, she'd stolen his heart. At first, he'd thought of her as another challenge. Life was full of them ten years ago. Instead, she'd been the only calm in his life. She'd soothed his anger at his father, at the people who didn't believe in him, she'd reveled in his successes in sports, she'd encouraged him to be more than even he'd thought was possible. She'd been his friend. His lover. His life.

Reluctantly he dragged his gaze away from womanly curves in snug jeans and a Western-style blouse. The diner was no longer all chrome and red vinyl but decorated in blue and beige with crisp, colorful curtains and tablecloths. Dark beige booths lined the walls, circling the round tables with their captain's chairs.

"Do you want to sit at the counter or—"

"There." He pointed to a table at the back of the café, a table where he'd etched their initials.

Leigh steadied herself as his gaze came back to her. She was twenty-seven, not seventeen. Whatever they'd shared was in the past. Somehow she'd act casual, friendly. "I'll get you a menu."

"It's a start."

Leigh knew then he hadn't changed. There was still a challenge, a curtness in his speech, a flicker of a dare in his eyes.

Ignoring stares, Jake settled on a chair against the window. Idly he glanced around the room, but his eyes swung back to her. He watched her smile at an elderly man. It was that warmth that had drawn him to her. She liked people, genuinely cared about them. Years ago, she'd come into his life when he'd needed someone who would listen. It had been one summer when he'd spent most of his time pumping gas at Bensen's Garage that he'd gazed down the street, hoping for glimpses of her through the windows of the diner.

Her father had been Sheriff Hal McCall. Her aunt had been married to Thomas Martin, the owner of the lumber mill and most of the commercial land in town. Leigh's friends had lived at the edge of town in old Victorian houses built on hills that towered with a superior view over the streets and the townspeople.

He was a Ryker, a boy whose father had been tagged the town drunk. He'd been a sullen, rebellious kid, smart in school but uncooperative. Nothing had been easy those days, especially private feelings for one girl. One summer night had changed everything. She'd been his. Leigh McCall had been his, had turned eyes bright with eagerness on him. When later she'd told him that she loved him, Jake Ryker had become king of the town, invincible. He nearly smiled at the thought. He'd been young and stupid, too, not to recognize that his beginnings would always shadow him in Pineview.

At the clatter of silverware, he looked to his left and made eye contact with Leigh's sister as she scooped up dirty cutlery from a table. He'd gone through school with Kathleen, while always eyeing her younger sister. Slim, she looked good, her strawberry blond hair cut fashionably short. "How are you, Kathleen?"

She gave him a quick laugh. "Mother of two now."

He smiled because she suddenly looked younger. "You're kidding?"

"Nope. And of course, they're little angels." Again, she laughed in the manner of someone pleased with her life.

Leigh watched the exchange, the easy smiles between her sister and Jake. His back braced against the wall, he looked as insolent, as brash as he had at nineteen. And as wonderful. The rough edges hadn't disappeared, but while he'd been broodingly handsome at nineteen, as if a storm brewed inside him, he carried an air of confidence now that heightened the toughness of his looks. This was still a man who barreled through life.

A menu tucked under her arm, Leigh rounded the counter. She supposed one man in the hospital with a cast on his leg should be grateful for that quality in his rescuer.

Drawn not by sound, but by the scent of a perfume that had haunted him for a decade, Jake followed her easy stride toward him. "That was quite a storm last night."

Leigh set the open menu on the table. "August storms always are." Nerves—she could hear them in the unsteadiness of her voice.

He'd thought he'd feel anger at her. Not only hadn't she waited for him, she'd also married another. But with her standing so near, he felt only a need to touch her again. "I remember."

It was instinctive. Their eyes met, and she could tell he, too, was thinking about one special summer's evening, when two young bodies had strained against each other for the first time. All the vulnerability of that August night years ago was with her again, as if the intervening years had never existed.

Tense, she wanted to get away from him and escape what only he had ever made her feel. But whispers buzzed around her. All her life, she'd lived in this town. She knew the people, knew if she lingered at his table, if she talked to him in the manner of old friends, she'd douse the rumors instead of fueling them. Seeing his bandaged hand, she asked, "Did you get that last night."

"Must have grabbed a piece of metal wrong," he said.

"You should have gone to the hospital right away."

The small talk annoyed him. At one time, they'd bared their souls to each other. "It's not that bad. What were you doing there?"

"I volunteer at the hospital one night a week to go out on calls." Discreetly Leigh ran a sweaty palm down her denim thigh. "Everyone volunteers for something. Don't you remember?"

He remembered the night volunteers had raced toward the fire at the feed-and-grain store where his father had worked. He remembered later all the anger and accusations. "What happened to the drivers?"

"They took X rays of the one man. He was released this morning from the hospital. The other driver is in a leg cast, and he'll be there another day. It could have been a much sadder day for their families."

"That part of the highway has always been dangerous."

She directed a smile at him that she hoped didn't look as tight as it felt. "Everyone was talking this morning. You're being called a hero."

That amused him. "I've been called a lot more and a lot worse by most of the people in this town."

Leigh expected the coolness she heard in his voice. Though the townspeople were friendly, honest and hardworking, they judged quickly. That Jake's father had spent time in prison and had never stopped causing the town trouble had led the way to their preconceived notions about his son. "Some of them have mellowed."

For some reason, he believed her. "That's good to know."

Hundreds of questions barraged her mind. There was so much left unsaid, so much that *couldn't* be said. "Have you decided what you want?"

He'd always known exactly what he wanted. "Just coffee."

"Be right back." Leigh took another order before she went to the coffee brewer. She wasn't a child anymore, harboring dreamy visions of being the woman who tamed him. She'd married a man who'd symbolized everything good. She'd grown up and understood now that the dark, dangerous man was only wonderful in a woman's fantasy. While she'd keep her manner friendly, she wouldn't forget that she'd believed in him and his promises, and he'd left without a care that he'd broken all of them. "Here you are," she said with an ease she didn't feel.

He looked away from the blue mug to her bare ring finger. "I'd heard you'd gotten married."

"I'm a widow now." She managed to say the words smoothly. They always seemed strange to her because they conjured up an image of a woman with gray hair, someone who'd spent decades instead of only months with her husband.

"Did I know him?"

Because she was afraid she might see hurt in his eyes, she concentrated on pouring the coffee. "He was my dad's deputy. Ken Grentham."

Jake remembered him well. They'd had words more than once, and always about Leigh. Grentham had baited him, feeling cocky with the blessing of Leigh's father.

"Children?" It took effort to ask.

"No." Leigh gauged how much to say as emotion flooded her. "I lost one."

No one knew better than him how much that loss had hurt. She loved kids. "Bad times."

Leigh nodded, grateful he hadn't offered sympathy. "Did you marry?"

"Not me." At that moment, he realized he'd have been satisfied with just feeling the silkiness of her hair beneath his fingers. "I was engaged once." It had been a foolish time in his life. He'd worked so hard to convince himself that another woman meant as much to him as Leigh had. The deception had lasted two weeks. He'd known he was fooling himself. There had been one woman for him—only one—her. He'd bowed out of the commitment, left Michelle the ring and an apology. "It didn't work out."

Nothing was ever so simple, but she didn't want to know more. Only one question really needed answering. "Are you here for long?"

"I don't know." Cautiously he sipped the steaming brew. "After my father died, there was some business to settle."

"No one knew where you were to send sympathy cards, but I am sorry." Leigh watched his brow lift in derision and wished she could tell him that she'd meant those words, but she doubted he'd believe anyone was sorry about Leonard Ryker's death. "Where have you been?"

"Not far. Salt Lake." He'd wandered only far enough to get away from one man. "How's your father?" he asked, wondering at what moment he'd see Sheriff Hal McCall and have an overdue showdown with him.

Only someone deaf wouldn't have heard the sarcasm in his voice. Leigh couldn't blame him. Her father had been hard on him. She'd always thought of him as a fair man and had always neatly buried any criticism about him. To her, her father could do no wrong. The apple of his eye, she had felt compelled to take his side. Even now, though he'd been dead for years, though her grief had been entombed in a secret part of herself, she wanted to come to his defense. "He was killed nine years ago."

Jake couldn't mouth phony words. He felt no grief at the news. He'd never liked the town's sheriff, but he knew Leigh had suffered and grieved for the loss of a father she'd loved and idolized.

"Do you want anything else?" Leigh asked with a nod at the menu.

It was a loaded question. "Nothing."

The sound of the bell announced the entrance of more customers. More bridge buddies of Grace's, they spotted Jake and their heads nearly collided as each one turned to whisper to the other. A step behind them, Mark entered, then charged toward her like some jealous protector.

"Did you hear this morning's newscast?" he asked, briefly casting a curious look at Jake. "Two men escaped from the Florence prison. One was a man named Fuller. The other was Randy Seaton, Leigh."

"Seaton? Are you sure?"

"I'm sure." Touching her arm, he pressured her to move away. "If you have time, I'd like to talk to you."

So did Jake. He wanted to know what the hell was wrong, why worry had flickered in her eyes with that news. Mostly, he wanted to know how important to her the man gripping her arm was.

"I don't believe it," Leigh said softly, ambling with Mark toward the counter.

"Neither do I." He glanced over his shoulder. "So that's Jake Ryker. Everyone is talking about him."

Involved in other thoughts, Leigh forced herself to focus on Mark. "What?"

A tall man, his brown hair conservatively cut, he eyed the cleanliness of a stool at the counter before settling on it. "From what I've heard, he shouldn't have come back. His kind isn't needed here."

His kind. Leigh smothered a quick surge of annoyance. "Why are you so critical? You don't even know him."

"He has a reputation."

She nearly laughed at the ridiculousness of the conversation. "For doing what?" Other than breaking her heart, he was guilty of nothing.

"People claim he was always in trouble."

Leigh stepped around to the opposite side of the counter. "Yes, he was. Really criminal stuff. He raced his motorcycle through town."

The line between his brows deepened noticeably. "Are you defending him?"

No matter what had happened between her and Jake personally, she knew he was an honest man. "He doesn't need defending. He didn't do anything."

"Other people feel differently." Almost possessively he linked his fingers with hers on the counter. "Most people don't go where they're not welcome."

Leigh eased her hand from his. She wished Randy Seaton thought that way. "Are you sure Seaton was one of the men who escaped?"

"Yes."

"It wouldn't be logical for him to come back here."

"Well, in case he does, you should take some precautions."

She gave a nod of agreement to soothe him and left to pick up an order of pancakes. Despite her bravado, she jumped at a bang behind her and whipped around.

She saw her uncle holding a tray of dirty glasses, his brow knitted with a frown. "What's wrong?" he asked.

At five foot seven, she stood eye-to-eye with him. A portly man with a thin thatch of gray, her uncle Matt had been a sympathetic shoulder for her and Kathleen most of their lives. Personable, a gentler spirit than her aunt or her father, he'd never said a word when years ago she'd snuck out of work to spend a few minutes with Jake at the gas station.

"Nothing." She summoned a bright smile to erase the concern in his eyes.

He glanced at Jake. "Are you sure?"

She wasn't surprised that he'd presumed Jake was somehow at fault. That was the way it had always been. If something went wrong, if there had been trouble, people automatically thought of a Ryker. "Positive."

Seeming satisfied, he picked up the money envelope. "Would you watch the register for me while I go to the safe?"

Keeping the smile she'd given him firm on her face, Leigh handed change to a customer. Logic counted for something, she told herself. If Seaton had any brains, he was probably already in another state.

"Did trouble come in the door a few minutes ago?"

Leigh jerked her head up at the familiar lazy drawl.

Jake resisted the urge to touch a strand of hair that had loosened from its barrette. "Who was that?"

She owed him no explanations, but she'd never been able to keep anything from him. For an instant, that thought frightened her. She had secrets now, one in particular she'd never expected to share with anyone but her family. "That was Mark Wendley," she finally responded. "The bank manager." She took the dollar he held in his fingers. Because she couldn't veil her worry, she saw no point in not telling him what was public knowledge. "Seaton—"

"The one who escaped?"

"Yes." Leigh handed him change. "He used to live here."

Jake frowned, searching his memory for the family name. "I don't remember him."

"He came here a few months after you left. My dad had a lot of trouble with him. Vandalism, petty theft. But it wasn't until after my father died that a lot of burglaries took place." She looked down to close the cash register drawer. "One night last year, I was at a community meeting about the Independence Day celebration. After it, while driving home, I saw Randy Seaton breaking into the Gafferty house."

Jake guessed what she hadn't said yet. "You were a witness against him?"

"Yes. The only one. After his trial, he threatened to come back and get even."

No one knew better than him that some threats had to be taken seriously.

"Jake Ryker, what a surprise," a grating high-pitched voice announced behind him.

Leigh noted Jake's grimace as Grace, with her sly smile and eagle eyes, waddled up close.

"Are you worried?" Jake asked, ignoring the woman who was practically breathing on the back of his neck.

Another time, another place, Leigh might have shared her apprehension. She couldn't talk about it to Kathleen or Uncle Matt and alarm them, but Jake... If things were different between them. But they weren't, she reminded herself. "I don't think he'll come here."

He caught the small show of nerves as she fingered the gold chain at her neck. Years couldn't dissolve the closeness that they'd shared. He knew her—he understood what made her smile and cry, what touched her heart and when she was warring with herself to stay calm. "I'm still a hell of a listener."

Yes, he had been. He'd sat quietly beside her at the lake while she'd rambled about school, complained about her aunt's interference in her life and expressed her youthful exasperation that her father was paying too much attention to Abby's condemnations of Jake. He'd held her when she'd felt lousy with PMS, let her cry when she'd lost a bid for student council president. He'd always been there for her—except when she'd needed him the most.

"Jake," the voice behind him insisted.

Briefly, in an old familiar way, he shot a quick, amused look at Leigh before he turned around. "Mrs. Newell, how are you?"

Like Leigh, she obviously expected him to level her with one of his don't-mess-with-me glares. Flabbergasted by his friendliness, the woman stammered, "Why—why I'm fine."

"That's good news."

As he stepped around her, she gaped after him.

Leigh, too, couldn't stop herself from staring at him. He had changed. Though confidence still marked his stride and an edge of defiance still lingered in his voice, in less than a second, she'd felt and seen a more congenial Jake Ryker.

Grace inched closer to the counter. "I don't care what kind of heroics he did last night," she whispered. "A leopard doesn't change his spots."

Leigh swore silently, weary that old prejudices persisted. She stifled a sharp return. Losing her temper wasn't her style. By nature, she searched for the best in people, overlooked hints of nastiness and rarely started an argument, because she never had the heart to stretch anger long enough to win one.

The silence paid off. Getting no response from her, Grace waddled toward the exit.

Rejoining Kathleen at the cook's counter, Leigh waited for an order.

"Interesting morning." With a curious sidelong look at her, Kathleen shoved bread into a toaster. "I think he's more handsome now."

In Leigh's mind, no man had matched him.

"And he still looks at you in the same way."

And he still unsettled her. Aware of Kathleen's inquisitive stare, she roused a grin. "Love is making you a drippy Pollyanna."

With a laugh, Kathleen stepped away with her order.

Leigh couldn't find anything laughable about her present situation. Filling coffee cups at the counter, she worked her way to the end to take Eddie Tobbins's order. "Coffee and a danish, as usual, Eddie?"

One of Pineview's deputies, he'd tried to get a date with her when he'd first arrived in town and she'd refused. He'd never taken the refusals personally. Like everyone else in town, he knew why he was off-limits to her. She'd lost two men who'd worked in law enforcement and had agonized over their unexpected and early deaths.

"Ryker sure stirs up this town," Eddie declared. "Everyone's talking about him. Doc said everyone who came in mentioned him. And—" leaning forward, he beckoned her closer to him and spoke low "—Doc said Ryker had more than just a sore hand. Doc said he's recovering from a bullet wound in the shoulder." With narrowed eyes, he reminded Leigh of Clint Eastwood. "Think I'll keep an eye on him. The way I figure it, there are only a couple of ways that someone gets shot. Clumsy handling of a gun, or running from the law. Unless—" he paused and sipped the coffee she'd set before him "—he's a cop."

He looked amused. She wasn't. She straightened her back, not thrilled with any of those possibilities.

Chapter Three

Jake considered what Leigh had told him about Seaton. There was no doubt in his mind that he shouldn't get involved, that she wouldn't want him to. But hell, he was a cop. It didn't matter that he was out of his jurisdiction. Like doctors, cops never went off duty.

After a trip down memory lane, past old haunts, he turned into the parking lot adjacent to the redbrick building that housed the sheriff's office. As he entered the monochrome beige room, he realized he'd never asked the name of the new sheriff. Like bookends, two deputies sat at desks on either side of a short, oak barricade with its swinging gate. The desk behind it was empty.

Jake knew both deputies. Al Deavers had been a junior when Jake had graduated. Bulky, he'd been assured a linebacker's spot on the high school varsity team in his sophomore year. The other deputy, a newcomer to town, was the one he'd met on the highway.

Slightly overweight now, with a receding hairline, Al tipped his head back and cast a dark look at Jake. "I heard you were back."

Jake read the silent message. We don't want trouble here. He wasn't a nineteen-year-old kid, and the law didn't scare the daylights out of him anymore. Working on the city's police force, he had more experience than either man before him.

It took only a mention about his job to change the mood in the room. Jake had counted on that. Cops belonged to a brotherhood of the badge that made acceptance automatic.

"I'll be damned," Al kept saying, shaking his head. "Who'd have thought you'd be a cop."

Eddie swiveled his chair away from his desk. "I heard you had a bullet wound."

"I'm on R and R for a while," Jake answered.

For the next ten minutes, he reminisced with Al about the good old days and Coach Jackson. Eddie swiveled his chair toward them, a captive audience to their anecdotes.

Laughing at Al's last comment, Jake eyed the clean desk behind the oak barricade. "Who took over after Hal McCall died? Who's your sheriff?"

Al scratched his jaw. "Don't have one."

"What do you mean, you don't have one?"

"We had a temporary here for a few months," Eddie piped in. "But then the burglaries started. People weren't too happy with him. He left. So now it's just me and Al.''

''Why wasn't one of you made sheriff?''

''I don't want it,'' Al said. ''Hell. Remember, I didn't even want to be a co-captain on the baseball team. And Abigail Martin isn't too keen about either of us.''

Jake knew her disapproval would be sufficient for the town council not to offer either of them the job.

Eddie shrugged. ''The job would be a real headache, especially now. Maybe Seaton won't show up,'' he said almost hopefully.

''That would suit me fine, too.'' Al rotated a pencil between his fingers like a baton. ''Did you come back to settle your father's business?''

Jake didn't bother to weigh his words carefully. ''That and to do some investigating. I want to see one of your old files.''

Jake didn't miss the meaningful look exchanged between them.

Al made a face. ''I don't think we can give it to you without an okay, Jake. The town council is our boss right now. Tell me what you want to look at.''

''It's a twelve-year-old case.''

Interested, Eddie scooted his chair closer. ''Why would you want to know about something that happened twelve years ago?''

Al didn't blink. He knew. Hell, everyone who'd been in town twelve years ago knew about the fire.

''I'm not even sure where it'll be.'' Al glanced at Eddie for confirmation. ''Probably in storage, huh?''

"Think so."

"Sheriff McCall cleared everything out of here years ago. When I started working with him and Ken, he'd already moved all of them. So I don't even know where that file is buried. But I'll have to check with the mayor and the rest of them first. I'll get back to you."

Minutes later, Jake strolled outside and slid into his Jeep. He'd counted on his badge earning him some professional courtesy.

Across the street, Leigh swept out of the diner. Before he left town this time, he'd have more than answers about that fire. He'd find out why the only woman he'd ever loved had chosen another.

Leigh whisked into the post office to mail a package, a gift for a friend's new baby, then strolled to the shoemaker's, with a pair of her uncle's shoes in a bag, nodding to neighbors ambling by. She had an hour to herself. She needed it today. Like a whirlwind, trouble had swept into her life. Randy Seaton's escape made her nervous, but she believed he'd be on his way to Mexico. He might not be a problem.

Jake was. All morning, she'd listened to gossip about the bullet wound in his shoulder. She didn't want to talk or think about him.

Deliberately she spent the hour alone, feeding the ducks at the pond in the center of town and closeting herself in an alcove at the library. By the time she returned to the diner, she'd relieved tension. She hurried behind the counter with an armful of paperbacks from the library. Guaranteed to be the quietest place in town, it was also the most relaxing.

Setting the books and the bag from Vin's Shoe Repair under the shelf at the back of the counter, she looked up in response to the excited buzzing of conversation.

From across the room, Kathleen beamed, then waved her left hand to flash the diamond on her ring finger.

Smiling, Leigh flew to her. "When? When did he give it to you?"

"Minutes ago."

"Oh, Kath." On a laugh, she hugged her sister. "I'm so happy for you." Leigh pulled back and held Kathleen by the shoulders. "Have you set a date?"

"Not yet."

"So tell me everything."

"Later." She grimaced in a comical way. "Someone wants to talk to you."

"Someone?"

Picking up a tray of drink orders, Kathleen jerked her head toward the office at the back of the diner. "Aunt Abby."

Leigh could think of only one reason for her aunt's unexpected visit. Steps from the office door, she paused and pasted a bright smile on her face. Dealing with her aunt always required enormous energy.

At sixty-five, Abigail Martin was plump and her hair snow-white, but she wasn't the sweet grandmotherly type. She always carried herself like a reigning monarch, and acted like one, too, Leigh mused as her aunt motioned with an elegant backhand toward the chair across the desk from her. "Sit down, Leigh."

For the life of her, she didn't know why she was feeling as if she were sixteen again.

"I've come because I'm concerned. Grace Newell was on my doorstep an hour ago to tell me that Jake Ryker is back in town."

Leigh braved her aunt's stare. "How considerate of her."

Abby arched a brow. "I doubt thoughtfulness was her intention. She felt compelled to tell me every lurid detail about your meeting with him in the diner."

Leigh cracked a smile. "Lurid? Nothing lurid happened."

"You weren't talking and smiling with him?"

Her dry, clipped tone reeked with disapproval. Leigh refused to play the game her aunt had started. "Yes, I talked to him."

"He's not back a day and already causing trouble."

"What has he done? He's only going to be here until he settles his father's business, so why don't we—"

Her aunt scoffed. "What business? Leonard Ryker had nothing. He wasted away all the money his father left him and amounted to nothing. By the time he died, he was a disgrace to the town."

Leigh weathered a rush of anger. "I don't know what business," she said to draw her aunt away from further disparaging words about Jake's father. She recalled the few times she'd been in Jake's home. Leonard had never spoken to her. She surmised that at one time he must have been a handsome man, but he'd looked haggard and angry when she'd seen him, content with the companionship of a bottle.

"Nothing has changed," her aunt returned sharply.

I have, Leigh thought. Intimidation no longer buckled her knees. "I'm sure he won't stay long." She rounded the desk to touch her aunt's shoulder reassuringly.

"You're not listening to me," her aunt flared. "He is bound and determined to cause trouble. He wants to see your father's report on that fire."

Leigh's hand stilled in midair.

"He has no right to see it. I won't have him questioning everything in your father's report." Her fingers tight on the pearl handle of her cane, she rose to stand beside Leigh. "If you felt loyalty for your father, you would feel the same way."

Though Leigh had never considered herself dense, she didn't understand her aunt. "He isn't going to question anything. Why would he?"

Piercing dark eyes zeroed in on Leigh. "Why do you think he wants to read it?"

"Probably to learn the truth. There was never any evidence against Leonard Ryker or he'd have been arrested. Everyone just speculated and assumed he was guilty of starting the fire," she said, speaking with candor about feelings she'd carried silently inside her for years. "Unfairly, some people in this town found Jake's father guilty when there'd been no proof he was."

"You were a child. You don't know what you're talking about."

"Then tell me."

Her aunt stiffened noticeably. "Don't let a handsome face fool you."

Moving with her to the doorway, Leigh touched her aunt's arm in a soothing gesture.

It proved futile. Anger oozed from the woman. "Like father, like son."

Leigh didn't believe that, but she thought something had to be done, and quickly. If her aunt was right, Jake would stir up old resentments and anger.

Leigh breezed into the diner and out again, telling Kathleen she'd be back in half an hour. It took nearly that long to find Henry Linser and learn which motel Jake was staying at.

Though searching for him would provoke gossip, whispers carrying her name seemed unimportant if she could stop the town from self-destructing.

The new two-story, crisp white motel overlooked the woods, offering guests a view of immaculately landscaped grounds. It was owned by Grace's brother. That Jake had chosen it seemed like a bad omen to Leigh.

She was right.

As she left the motel office and rounded the side of the building, she nearly plowed into Grace. Leigh went through the motions—a quick nod and a sunny smile—but never slowed her pace.

Three times she rapped on the motel door opposite the poolside while she geared up for an emotional roller coaster. When he didn't answer, she turned away, convincing herself it was for the best. Knowing Jake, he'd have listened to her rehearsed speech and ignored it.

"Looking for me?"

Head bent, hunting in her purse for her car keys, she nearly misstepped off the curb. A rag in his hand, he lounged against the fender of his Jeep. It was crazy, but she felt breathless.

"Bring a casserole?"

"What?"

"Isn't that the usual excuse for visiting someone new in town?" he asked while he wiped off the front window of his car.

"No casserole." She'd had everything planned when she'd marched toward his motel room. This wasn't how it was supposed to go. "I need to talk to you, Jake."

She surprised him by inching closer to lean against the hood near him. "What's this about?"

"My aunt."

Unconsciously Jake rubbed harder at a smudge on the glass. "Dear Aunt Abby."

Leigh took no offense. He had every right to feel some resentment toward her aunt. She'd been a ringleader in the campaign against the Rykers. It still behooved Leigh to know why, and no amount of questioning had ever produced anything except Aunt Abby's curt responses. "She told me earlier today that you want to see the file about the fire."

"I think I have a right to."

"Why are you doing this? You know it'll only stir up bad memories."

"Don't you think the truth is more important?"

"Of course it is." She wanted to appeal to him, but staring at the rigid set of his jaw, she knew better. "I wonder what you think you'll learn. Your father did threaten Duncan Wilder, swear to get even. Half a dozen people heard him make threats."

Jake shrugged a shoulder. "When he was drunk he didn't think straight. He said a lot of dumb things. After the fire started at Wilder's Feed and Grain, people were sure he'd started it. No one bothered to look for another suspect."

"People were angry, scared," she said, feeling compelled to defend her father and the people she'd known all her life. "Duncan Wilder was in the hospital, fighting for his life."

"I remember." He studied the dirty rag in his hand. "There were a lot of things about my father that I never liked, but he wasn't guilty that time."

Leigh sensed she was facing a brick wall. "Jake, I'm asking you to let this go."

His expression unyielding, he turned cold eyes on her. "Why?"

"Because people will get angry again. They don't forget or forgive easily here."

An old fury baited him. "Who are you protecting? Your family?"

Of course he'd think that. Her family had been at odds with his for as long as she could remember because of some unspoken feud. "Why would I need to?'' she asked with as much calm as she could muster. If they both lost their tempers, nothing would be gained. "They did nothing wrong."

"So sure of that?"

"Yes, I am."

"Then why worry about some report that's buried in the storage room?"

"I told you why." Leigh tried reasoning. "I care about the people who live here. I don't want to see this town divided again. Do you remember what it was like? Some people believed your father wasn't treated fairly because he lived on Weaver Road. There was anger that had nothing to do with truth. Class distinction divided this town. Do you want that to happen again?"

"I don't give a damn."

Annoyance bubbled inside her. She was grateful for it. She'd been feeling a familiar need to reach out to him. "Aren't you a little old to be playing tough guy?"

"That Ryker boy is a bad seed," he said almost mockingly.

Frowning, she nudged aside emotion that was teetering more toward compassion than she wanted. "I never thought so."

His back to her, he stretched into his Jeep for a pack of cigarettes on the dashboard.

"I saw a young man who went from bar to bar every night, looking for his father, taking him home so he wouldn't be found passed out in the street the next morning."

He didn't want her kindness or understanding. He wanted the truth. "Guess you'll have to make a choice."

His words pricked at her. She'd done that once and lost. She'd chosen him, believed in him, and he'd stripped her of even her pride. "Why do you insist on stirring up trouble?"

"Try and understand something," he said, so deadly serious that she felt a chill rush through her. "My father carried the stigma of being an arsonist. And your father didn't do a damn thing about clearing his name."

More than anything, she wanted to stop the explosiveness of the moment, and she couldn't. Hadn't her aunt already challenged her loyalty to her father? "People respected him. He'd get up in the middle of the night if someone needed him. My father was a good sheriff."

"To everyone, unless his last name was Ryker."

In her eyes, her father had been a kind man. If he'd had any weakness, it was his daughters. Raising them alone, he'd been overprotective, sometimes authoritative. "You have bad feelings about him. I understand some of them."

He raised a brow. "Some?"

"Yes, only some. He was right about us. He warned me to stay away from you, that you'd leave."

He said nothing. What could he say? He couldn't fight her memory of her father without hurting her more.

"He was a good man, a wise one." Gratefully her throat didn't freeze anymore when she talked about him. "He warned Kathleen, too. He told her not to marry Larry. She did, and she was left to raise two children by herself," Leigh said, wishing he'd believe what she did. "I'm sure he made mistakes, but he wasn't dishonest. And that's what you want to prove, isn't it?"

"I didn't say he was guilty of anything."

"Except not looking for the truth." She met his eyes steadily now, even as she was aware that if she stared too long at him her blood would warm. "And you're going to stay and try to clear your father's name, no matter who you hurt."

"*My* name," he said in a voice laced with quiet anger. "I lived with what people said about him."

More than anyone, she'd witnessed how much he'd carried the weight of his father's wrongdoing on his shoulders. But she'd never believe what he was implying about her father.

"If you're so sure about your father, prove me wrong."

With words and a look, he challenged her. It was Jake Ryker at his best. "I'm not going to, Jake." At one time, she'd have agreed to anything he wanted. She was stronger now.

His mouth tightened almost to a sneer. "Did your aunt send you here?"

"No, she didn't send me. I came on my own." Leigh watched the breeze tousle his dark hair. "Why would you think that?"

"Because she's no fool. She'd know you're the one person who could talk me out of something."

Leigh frowned as his words made too much sense. Had she been manipulated? Had her aunt counted on her coming to him to persuade him to change his mind?

Lazily, he dragged his eyes from her to light a cigarette. "You're not sure now, are you?" Calmer, he smiled wryly. "She's shrewd, Leigh. She knows that the best way to break the enemy is to find his weak spot."

"I never thought you had any," she said honestly.

"She knows what it is." He smiled again then, slowly, a little amused. "You."

Like before, she felt caught in the middle. "Why can't we all forget the past?" she asked in a wistful tone.

Jake steeled himself against the hint of an appeal brimming her voice. Blowing out a stream of smoke, he wanted to shake her, make her choose him over everyone else. "Some of it, I don't want to. But I'll think about what you said."

A concession of sorts, she realized, feeling unsteady as she ambled back to her car. She unlocked the door but didn't slide in, just as Eddie whipped into the parking space beside her.

In a rushed movement, he slid out of the cruiser and stood beside his open door. "I was hoping I'd find you. Seaton was spotted by a camper about five miles from here."

His business or not, Jake rounded the front of his Jeep and bridged the distance to her. "When?"

"About half an hour ago we got the bulletin," Eddie answered.

After what Eddie had said in the diner, Leigh had expected him to play Dirty Harry with Jake. Puzzled, she tried to understand more than what Eddie was telling them.

"We're going to get some help from the highway patrol. They'll put up roadblocks in case he hitches a ride, and we're going to start hunting for him around here."

At the anxiousness in his voice, Leigh was forced to pay closer attention. Until that moment, she hadn't believed Seaton would stay so close to town.

"So, you be careful." Eddie swung a look at Jake. "With only me and Al here, we could use someone else to guard her."

Leigh cast a puzzled look at Eddie, then at Jake. "Guard me?"

"Now, don't get all upset," Eddie soothed. "What I meant is if we need it," he added as an afterthought.

He said something else before sliding back in his cruiser. She didn't hear it. Her ears hummed as her breath locked in her throat. With her eyes downward, she mulled over everything she knew. Like pieces of a giant jigsaw puzzle, everything started to fall into place. Doc had examined a bullet wound in Jake's shoulder. Eddie was sharing information with Jake. People were acting like the town's hellion had sprouted a halo. Why seemed suddenly obvious. "You're a cop," she said softly, as if speaking to herself. Just the sound of that word knotted her stomach.

Jake ground out his cigarette. He'd have had to be deaf not to hear the incredulity in her voice. "Is it that hard to believe?" he asked, annoyed that her lack of belief in him hurt.

She sent him a humorless smile. She could have re-assured him. She knew the honesty, the strength, the courage he possessed. But why? Why had another man she cared about chosen to walk on the edge of danger? "I have to go back to work now." To say more would have been stupid. He wouldn't under-stand her feelings; no one would unless they'd walked in her shoes.

Turning away, Leigh saw Grace's nose pressed to the motel office window. By morning, it would be all over town that she'd visited Jake at his motel.

She'd been wrong. At nine that evening, she wan-dered with Kathleen into the living room of the Phil-lips house for a demonstration party. Colorful plastic kitchenware had been stacked on top of the lace ta-blecloth in the dining room.

As more women drifted in, conversation raised to deafening proportions. Emmy Phillips regaled every-one with the ingredients of a prizewinning peach chif-fon pie. Al's wife, LeeAnn, carried on about her youngest child's talent at ballet, and seated nearby, the Pearly sisters, twins, chatted about a trucker who'd dated both of them at one time or another.

Next to Leigh, Arlene Banner scowled at the pink punch in the imitation crystal cup. "I'm leaving this town someday. As soon as I get enough money saved." She laughed at herself. "I'll probably be old and feeble by then, but I'm going." She smoothed fingers along the side of her blond hair, cut and styled at Sallie's Beauty Salon to resemble a picture she'd seen in the salon window. "What about you?" she asked, her eyes sweeping over Kathleen and Leigh.

"I'm content," Kathleen said between bites of a homemade sugar crisp.

Everyone who overheard laughed.

"Why not?" Marianne Pearly said. "You're sporting a rock on your finger."

"Leigh?" Arlene insisted.

She'd never thought of leaving. Others might have grander aspirations, but being a waitress suited her. She liked people, enjoyed laughing at Clyde's old jokes, and felt secure in the place she'd been born and raised. "I couldn't imagine walking down a street and not having someone say hello to me."

"But a bigger city like, say, Salt Lake . . . ?"

Leigh slanted a wary look at her, sensing the direction of Arlene's conversation. "From what I heard, you'd know someone there," she added not too subtly about Jake.

For the umpteenth time, during lulls in conversation, everyone swung expectant looks at her.

"I've had it," Marianne said. "Tell us about him before I die of curiosity."

"I heard you were at his motel," Arlene added.

Motor-mouth Grace had struck again, Leigh reflected. "What's to tell. He's a cop now."

"We know that. Mayor Tebner said he checked. I think no one believed it, and that's why he did. But Marvin said Jake's got a bunch of commendations. So we know that's true. But what about him? Other than being more gorgeous than he was before, has he changed?"

"Ladies." A wide-hipped woman with dark hair demanded their attention and held up a green plastic container. "This is our lettuce crisper."

Leigh shoved a cookie in her mouth, grateful someone else was the center of attention. Restless, she indulged in a slice of chocolate cake and two more cookies while she listened halfheartedly to the woman's spiel. But her thoughts drifted. The past meant nothing. Ten years ago, Jake had made a decision to live his life without her. Today, knowing he'd gone into law enforcement, she had no trouble accepting that they would always be wrong for each other.

Chapter Four

A cool night's breeze fluttered over Jake's damp skin. Amazingly, three drivers had honked from their cars in passing as he'd jogged back toward the motel.

His sneakered feet hitting the cement at the edge of the pool, he shook his head in amusement and disbelief. This evening he'd shared coffee and conversation with Al and had nearly choked on the former when the mayor had given him a cheery hello. As he was walking down the street, two of the town council members had stopped him with a reminder about the upcoming Founder's Day celebration. And when he'd entered Melbourne Drugs to buy razor blades, old man Melbourne had strolled down the aisle with him to show him the best buy instead of throwing him out.

Winded, Jake slowed his pace to cool down and wiped the back of his hand across a sweaty brow before opening the door to his motel room. They were all dazed from the heat, he decided, unable to imagine another explanation.

Minutes later, showered and dressed, he peered through the blind slats at the pizza parlor across the street. People described him as a loner. *Lonely* fit better. Friends from the precinct had occupied his time. He dated regularly, bowled once a week, enjoyed a monthly poker game, even accepted friends' hospitality at family barbecues, but something had been missing from his life.

He'd never forgotten one young girl; he'd only delegated her memory to some secret slot in his brain. Now she was with him again, every memory so vivid he felt the aching, the yearning for her smiles, her laughter, her kiss.

With an oath, he moved quickly out the door and across the street. Dumb thinking did more harm than good. He entered the pizza parlor, and as if time had stood still, the familiar smell of tomato sauce loaded with garlic greeted him. From a corner of the room, Alabama blared from the jukebox. And, slouched in a corner booth, an old buddy raised a beer glass to him and grinned.

Don Ansger had been a studious kid in high school, an outsider and a kindred soul. Though he'd never quite fit in during the "good old days," he'd become a part of the establishment, he explained after Jake joined him. He taught mathematics at the high school now, and through a body-building program, he'd undergone a metamorphosis from a ninety-pound weakling to a lean Arnold Schwarzenegger look-alike.

Over a pepperoni pizza and a pitcher of beer, they played catch-up about the town.

Don sprinkled Parmesan cheese on another slice of pizza. "This business about Seaton sure is something, isn't it?"

Jake downed half his beer. "Were you around when he was on trial?"

"Sure was," he mumbled between bites. "Everyone crowded the courthouse from start to finish."

His hunger fading, Jake lit a cigarette. "Did you hear his threat?"

"People in the next county could have heard it. He acted like a crazy man, spitting the words out, pulling away from the deputies and lunging at Leigh. Scared the daylights out of all of us." He shook his head slowly. "She must be spooked now."

"You wouldn't know it to talk to her."

"She's a strong woman. It wasn't easy for her, losing her father and her husband at the same time."

Jake set his forearms on the table and hunched closer. "How did that happen?" It was a question he couldn't have asked her.

"Sheriff McCall was on highway duty and stopped a car for speeding. The two in the car were wanted for armed robbery. There was a shooting. One deputy was wounded. The sheriff and the other deputy, her husband, were killed." He paused to sip his beer. "I don't know how she handled it. Three months before that she'd lost the baby.''

Jake looked away, feeling his stomach clench. There was no escaping what gnawed at him. She'd offered even that part of their dream to another man. "How old was the baby?"

For a long moment, Don stared at the pine table. "Uh . . . I think she was eight months pregnant when it happened."

Jake wanted to stay angry but couldn't. All he could think about was the depth of her agony. During quiet nights when they'd been alone, she'd fantasized about the children she'd have, the family they'd raise.

"I thought you two were meant for each other."

Jake watched him devour another slice. "So did I," he said quietly.

One white daisy on the hood of her car the next morning and Leigh felt her world tilt. Only one man knew that was her favorite flower.

Leigh stalked to her car, snatched up the flower and whirled around. She had no excuse for keeping it, for setting it in a bud vase on her kitchen table. She simply couldn't throw it away. Or forget about it.

Because she believed in reasoning her way out of difficulties, she assured herself it was logical to still feel something for Jake. Every woman clutched close, in some hidden part of herself, memories of every first in her life. And he'd been the first male to make her feel like a woman. That memory was bound to stay with her, she told herself as she roared down the road that led into town. But had he ever thought about her after he'd left? Did he care that she'd wept for him?

Throughout the day, an edgy mood nagged at her. Unable to shake it, Leigh attacked a bag of parsley, separating sprigs with fervor. It didn't help that the diner was empty. Business had slowed by six, and most of the regulars had joined the crowd gathered at the high school. As a celebration, the softball tournament came a close second behind the Fourth of July in Pineview, since a majority of the male population competed in it.

Having completed her last task of the day, Leigh decided to abandon her usual method for alleviating stress—going home, soaking in a hot tub and reading a book. She needed noise, people, a diversion from her own thoughts.

Joining Kathleen on one of the jammed bleachers, Leigh sipped her soda while covering one ear to block out Kathleen's yell of encouragement to her "honey." Jim rubbed his feet into the dirt for the third time, like a bull getting ready to charge, then swung and missed. It was the bottom of the ninth inning, and the two strikes against him stirred excitement and shouts of advice from the spectators.

"I'm going down there," Kathleen said, bounding from the bleachers.

Retrieving a candy bar from her purse, Leigh thought her sister was already *too* much distraction, but didn't bother to stop her. At the crack of the bat, she gave it her all, offering her voice to the roar of the

crowd. A loud collective sigh merged with cheers as
Jim slid into third.

With the next batter's appearance at home plate,
Leigh descended the bleachers to return to the diner
for the after-game crowd. At the backstop, she
watched the batter hit a fast line drive between second and third. Around her, the crowd yelled for Jim,
who raced toward home plate. He beat the ball by one
step, rocking the bleachers.

Smiling, Leigh pivoted away and found herself face-
to-face with Jake. Instinctively, every nerve in her
body sprang to attention.

"Who were you rooting for?"

"Bates Construction." The wind tossed her hair.
She didn't touch it even when strands flew across an
eye. She wanted to keep moments between them casual, but every second with him tumbled her back in
time. And she wished— God, she wished everything
was different. "I had little choice," she said on an easy
laugh that carried more nervousness than humor.
"Kathleen wouldn't forgive me if I wasn't loyal to the
team Jim's playing on."

As she raked fingers through tangled strands, Jake
wanted to stop her, because it looked wild, the way he
remembered it after it had been mussed by his hands.
"Jim's her husband?"

"Her husband left. You didn't know him. But she's
heading to the altar for a second time with Jim Baylor." She caught herself rambling and didn't bother to
add that Jim was the head mechanic at a dealership
near the edge of town.

To keep from touching her, he hooked his fingers into the front pocket of his jeans. "It was a close game."

"They could have used you. You used to be the best third baseman this town had."

As spectators crowded around them, she made a move forward, preceding him. Despite her efforts to inch her way past people on the sidewalk, twice they were stopped. Neighbors greeted him hesitantly but not coolly. He thought of his last summer in town, when he'd played in the tournament, showing off for her. They'd drawn stares and whispers then, too. "I expected goodbye, good riddance."

"They didn't understand you," she said when they were clear of the crowd. "You were angry a lot then. And rebellious."

"Your father said good riddance."

She couldn't deny what they both knew was the truth. "He was afraid you'd lead me astray."

"I did," he said lazily.

Nerves danced like a warning. Leigh quickened her stride as she directed their path down the alley behind the diner. "Why are you so sure your father wasn't responsible for that fire?"

Jake followed her lead for the moment. "Not because I don't think he'd do something like that," he assured her. "But I saw my old man passed out in Bill Kiley's cornfield the night of the fire. I was taking him home when the fire started."

"He had an alibi," she said, rather than asked. "Did my father know that?"

"Sure. He didn't believe me, but because of me they couldn't arrest him."

Confusion stopped her from reaching for the handle on the back door. She didn't want to believe what he was saying, but the Jake she'd known had never been a liar. "None of this makes sense."

He could have argued, but discerned she wasn't ready to face the truth. "Some things don't," he said to ease her mood.

There had to be some reason for her father's actions that Jake wasn't aware of.

Hearing a meow, Jake smiled at the calico cat slithering around a trash can toward a water bowl. "Your cat?"

Leigh leaned over to stroke its furry back. "George." She tucked a finger behind the cat's ear and scratched. "I always wanted one. But my father had allergies."

"He'd disapprove of you taking in a stray."

Leigh straightened. "How do you know the cat was one?"

"You always were a sucker for an outcast, Leigh."

In the dim light of the streetlight, she noted a smile in his eyes. She'd seen the look before when he'd been poised above her, his lips a hairbreadth from her, his eyes smiling in the same way as he'd laughed. Aching with love, she'd smoothed back hair that had been cut rebelliously long then. And they'd loved. In the middle of a meadow of sunflowers near the lake.

She gave her head a small shake to shut out the memory. So easily he could lull her like before. A whisper, a smile, a caress—anything could throw her off-balance. "You left the flower, didn't you?"

"Did you keep it?"

"You knew I would. But..." Inwardly she tried to relax. "Don't give me any more."

As she started to turn away, he closed his fingers over her wrist. "Are you all talk, Leigh?"

The fingers on her were stronger than she remembered.

"Jake Ryker isn't good enough for you, is he?"

She couldn't believe he'd even ask that. "You know that isn't true."

"Then what is?"

"I don't like explosions in my life."

Idly his gaze roamed over her face. "You flatter me," he said, but he didn't think she'd meant to. Tempted, Jake toyed with the hair near her ear. Soft, sweet smelling, the fiery strands fell around his fingers, luring him to bury his face in them.

They couldn't go back. Didn't he realize that? Maybe they'd have had a chance at one time, but not now. "I don't date the law, Jake."

A moment passed before her words registered. Jake dragged his eyes away from the coppery strands entangling around his fingers.

"I learned my lesson. I've already lost two men who wore a badge. My father's and Ken's deaths were something I wasn't prepared for." Just talking about that time stirred an ache for those she'd lost. "I told you once that I had never understood my mother. I used to watch her pace if my father was even a few minutes late. I thought she was a nervous woman while he was so calm, but I wonder now if she really was, or if she became that way after she'd married him, after she'd realized how much risk there was in his job.''

"No one gets guarantees.''

He didn't understand the fear that shadowed not only the person who taunted danger, but also his loved ones. "Why? Why did you become a cop? Because it's exciting? Because you like walking the edge of danger?" Leigh met his eyes. "At any cost?''

He released a laugh that held no humor. When he'd first joined the police force, he'd fantasized about the moment when he told her, certain she'd be proud of him. "Be glad that some people think that way.''

"Oh, I'm grateful for every policeman and fireman there is," she said honestly. "I simply don't want one in my life.''

As much as she claimed his occupation bothered her and he understood why, he sensed she hadn't forgiven him for leaving her ten years ago. He thought they both deserved some explanations; now wasn't the time. They needed to find each other first.

Weary, Leigh started to step away. "I'd better—'' His palm near her shoulder, his breath fanning her cheek, he leaned forward until only inches separated them. How could she have believed that it would be simple to be casual with him? He'd been the love of her life, the only one.

She pressed a hand to his chest to stop him. But it was all with her again—the excitement and the heat. The shiver of response from his touch, the intense pull.

She should have pushed him away; she didn't.

She should have slipped free of his embrace; she couldn't.

As his mouth lowered and brushed hers once, and then again, as if testing, she gave in. One kiss, she mused, closing her eyes. Yes, one. Whether she was tempting fate or not, she would like to know if she'd remembered his kiss as more wonderful than it was.

A sigh escaped from her throat as his breath warmed her mouth. This was what she'd been longing for, what she was afraid of. The taste that aroused not only the memories but also the feelings.

There was such pleasure. It swept a heat over her that was dangerously close to smothering her. An ache rose and intensified. It, too, was the same. With their lips clinging, they were drifting back in time. With one kiss, he reminded her of the madness she'd known with no one else. Familiar sensations seemed to dissolve all the years they'd been apart. Her fingers curling into the material of his shirt, she responded in a way too much like before, savoring the play of his lips, answering the moist heat of his tongue, yearning for the demand and passion that she knew would surely come. She wanted to feel nothing. Instead, she realized how empty her life had been.

The mouth beneath his was as sweet as he remembered. He felt a need to drive her senseless, to make her pay for every moment he'd grieved for her. He couldn't. He gentled the kiss, taking care, knowing the treasure he was possessing. Her heart pounding against him, he yearned to savor and rediscover every sensation, but he felt her drawing back, insisting on ending what he felt he'd barely sampled.

Breathless, Leigh turned her mouth from his.

He stared at her bent head, wanting her. Hell, he wasn't sure but he thought he'd never stopped loving her. She'd been everything soft and gentle in his life. The only thing that ever was. "This time could be different."

Frightened, Leigh swung away, offering her back to him.

"A lot different," he murmured as he pressed his lips to the side of her neck.

With a soft moan, she closed her eyes and rested her forehead against the door. Too much time with him, and she'd lose. "Please, don't do this."

He was more patient now. He'd learned to be. He'd come back, expecting her to be married, planning to keep his distance. But the plan had changed. "Ten years ago, I was young—uncertain. No," he said, touching her shoulder and making her face him, "I was afraid to stand up for what I wanted. I'm not anymore. I want you."

No amount of reasoning would help. No strategy mattered. Unsteady, she stepped away and into the diner. With one kiss, he'd made her long to say those words back to him.

Chapter Five

Despite her morning off, Leigh had awakened earlier than usual. Usually she liked sleeping in, lazing around the house in her sleepwear, eating fruit while she read the newspaper, sometimes watching a movie video.

This morning, nerves plagued her. She'd eaten a grapefruit, dressed and then labored to concentrate on the Pineview editor's commentary about the upcoming Founder's Day and tourism being the town's livelihood.

Cradling a cup of coffee, she stared out the backdoor window. Sunlight danced across grass that needed mowing and spiked through the woods behind her house.

The garden beckoned her. When she'd been a child, her father had spent his spare time weeding and replanting the flowers that his wife had loved. With his death, Leigh had taken over the duty.

This morning, she needed quiet time to sort through muddled thoughts. Stepping outside, she adjusted the baseball cap on her head and knelt down to pull weeds. She'd been honest with Jake when she'd told him nothing that he'd said about the fire had made sense to her. For that matter, she'd been honest about everything.

With the garden shovel, she dug around the roots of one sturdy weed in her daisies that stretched stubbornly into the zinnias. The roots seemed to go on forever, and she wondered whimsically if some love was like that.

Immediately irritated, she yanked at the weed. Why couldn't she stop thinking about him? Maybe what she needed to do was list reasons why she didn't want him back in her life.

On her knees, she shifted and scooted forward. Start with the biggies. First, he'd left her without a good-bye. Despite all their plans, he'd simply disappeared from her life one night. If he'd loved her, he wouldn't have.

Second, he was a cop. She recalled only too well the waiting her mother had endured whenever her father had been late or called out in the middle of the night because someone had heard a prowler or a security alarm had been tripped. She'd suffered enough through that kind of waiting herself.

Third ... Leigh frowned, stymied. There had to be other reasons. He liked pretzels; she liked popcorn. That didn't qualify. Neither did his propensity for speed and her inclination toward slowness. They weren't true opposites. They'd shared so many things in common. They'd rarely argued, because they'd always been able to talk out a problem until—

Maybe she'd never understand why he'd left her, but she knew there were no other reasons. Traitorously her eyes veered to the back-porch swing where she'd sat with Jake so many nights after her father had gone to bed. The dreams and hopes for the future they'd shared had always included them being together.

Two reasons were enough, she decided, giving another yank on the weed. With satisfaction, she held it up and examined the monster roots. Determination was all it took to pull it. Determination would free her of Jake, too.

The smug, reassuring thought lasted only an hour. Dressed in jeans and a new Western-style blouse—a blue plaid with studs—Leigh ambled out the door, feeling stronger. In less than the time it took to draw a breath, all the resistance she'd gathered withered away.

Leaning against his car, sunlight highlighting the hint of red in his dark hair, Jake ground out a cigarette with the heel of his boot. Squinting against the morning glare, his eyes never strayed from her. "You're heading for work?"

Everything had seemed so easy, so sensible earlier. Leigh took the safest route to avoid his eyes. She slid on sunglasses more as a shield from his gaze than from the warm August sun. "Yes."

"Take a ride with me first."

Her fingers tightened on the leather of her shoulder bag. It would be insane to say yes.

"A short ride. I'm heading toward the house."

She knew going home wouldn't be easy for him. Not fair, she wanted to scream as she pictured him alone and facing some terrible memories. No matter what her mind told her, her heart, sometimes too compassionate toward others' pain, ruled. "I have to be at work in half an hour."

"I'll have you there on time." Pushing away from the Jeep, he rounded it and swung open the passenger door for her. "Scout's honor."

Leigh hustled around the back of the car as if she had no choice. "You were never a Scout."

The wind whistled through the Jeep as he whipped around a corner and onto the tree-lined road that led into Main Street. In the distance, towering mountains with staggered peaks stretched like an impenetrable wall to the east of the town.

Gazing at the trees blurring past, she smelled the faint hint of the nearby river. So much had changed and yet so little. A ride with him should have been safe, but each mile prompted memories about other times like this—driving down a familiar road, singing along with a favorite song on the radio, feeling the thrill of being with the one she wanted.

It was nonsense to remember anything, except that, like before, he would leave again. What she might never understand is why he had the first time. Had he sought something he couldn't find in town, some goal or dream he'd never shared with her? "What did you do after you left town?"

Easing up on the gas, he drove across the railroad tracks. For months after he'd left town, he'd drifted, looking for a job. He'd fantasized then that when he called Leigh, she would turn her back on everyone to join him. It was a silly daydream, one he'd clung to even after he'd learned she'd slipped away from him and into another man's arms. But he'd needed some goal, even one that was beyond his reach. At least, he'd thought it was. But here he was back in the town he'd sworn never to return to, and here she was sitting beside him, her perfume filling his senses with every breath he drew.

He kept his eyes on the road, alert to the children playing kick ball on the straggly grass of one front yard. "I did odd jobs for a while, then I attended night school. The pay wasn't great, but because I was alone, I didn't need a lot." He was being honest. After that phone call to his father, there had been no one to think about but himself. By the time his first year of college had ended, he'd had direction. Police work had filled a void. During those days at the police academy, he'd found what he'd been looking for. He was part of a family. It was—had always been—the missing element in his life.

Leigh frowned out the window with more questions. Why had he wanted to be alone? Had he thought she'd be a hindrance? Had he lied when he'd said he loved her? She'd never ask those questions. Her pride wouldn't allow it.

Her gaze strayed to the children playing, to one little boy with dark hair and an infectious grin. Would her child have looked like that now? All she'd been certain about was the dark hair, a grin that warmed the soul. She placed a hand against her stomach, wondering if the memory of the baby she'd carried, of the fluttering inside her, would ever not stir pain.

When the house he'd been raised in came into view, he slowed the Jeep to a crawl. A stranger's eye might think the clapboard cottage, with its small square windows, looked worn because of neglect, but the building had always borne the weathered gray look, had always needed painting.

"I'll go in alone," he said, braking in front of it. His work took him to sleazy places, where the smell of garbage permeated the air, where hookers' perfume nauseated passersby. He thought it ironic that he'd never really escaped the dingy atmosphere of his beginnings.

"I don't mind going," Leigh said softly.

He shrugged as if there were no problem. "I'll only be a few minutes." Quickly he strode through the overgrown grass before a wave of hesitation changed his mind.

Years rolled back at him as he climbed the sagging steps to the porch. The middle one was loose, always had been. The door squeaked open, and from the doorway, he took in the whole house with one sweeping glance: the chipped stove, the small yellowed refrigerator, the green sofa with its sagging cushions that Jake had slept on even during the years when he was too long for it.

Only vaguely he remembered his mother, a thin woman with light brown hair who'd looked tired all the time—a woman who had deserved better.

In no mood to linger, he crossed to the far wall and squatted to open the pull-down door of a cubbyhole storage area. Inside he found the one box that belonged to him.

The box held treasures of his youth. It amazed him that his father hadn't tossed out everything. Jake flipped open the carton's flaps and grinned at the sight of baseball trophies and a high school letter. Beneath it were a handful of photographs taken at the lake, in the snow—all of them with Leigh.

Nothing else was important. He stuffed the photos in his pocket and closed the carton. He'd always believed that reminiscing wasted time, that memories were best forgotten, that the past meant nothing if the future was empty. But would everything have been different if he'd stayed? He doubted it. He'd been gone ten years, and he still carried the stain of being Leonard Ryker's son.

He shut the door of the storage area, pushed to a stand and crossed the room. Halfway to the door, he caught himself walking softly. Old habits die hard, he realized. In his youth, he'd snuck out repeatedly, making sure he didn't wake his father. Dazed from alcohol, he'd always awaken angry, swinging his fist.

At the door, he paused. The imagination played games, for he could almost see his father sleeping on the green chair, hear his snores. The old man had never meant much to him, but for the sake of his name, Jake couldn't ignore questions about a fire that had happened twelve years ago.

Ascending the steps, he felt the old buried anger, the same anger that had stirred when during his childhood he'd longed for something as simple as a bike, and the old man had wasted the money on booze.

Early morning sunlight glaring in her eyes, Leigh raised a hand, shading them to see him better. Back straight, he walked as if he were returning from a leisurely stroll, but joining her in the Jeep, he didn't speak. She couldn't let him brood now anymore than she had before. "You're empty-handed."

"Nothing there," he said flatly, turning the key in the ignition. "There never was."

Her heart went out to him. Beneath the controlled, tough, almost world-weary exterior of this man, there was a vulnerable interior. Unfairly he'd carried a burden during an age of innocence. Inside the house, had he remembered the taunts, the disgrace, the humiliation that he'd never deserved? She wanted to wrap her arms around him. She wanted to tell him to forget the past. Forget the hurt. "Are you okay?"

He knew now why he'd asked her to come with him. It was her softness, her gentleness, he'd needed most at the moment. "I thought it would be easier," he admitted.

In silence, he drove the Jeep back along the same route. With a walk through the house, he'd realized that he could spend his lifetime traveling from one end of the globe to the other, but he'd never get far enough away to shed the coat of shame he'd worn as a child. "I always wondered if he was different when he was younger."

Leigh shifted on the seat toward him. It seemed strange they'd never talked about his father's youth before this. So much had been shared, but she'd always treaded cautiously, letting him lead the conversation about his father. "He wasn't in prison long, was he?" she asked, reaching out to him as the friend she'd once been.

"My mother said he was sentenced to five years for stealing, but they paroled him early. She knew him before he was arrested. I don't know why she loved him."

Leigh longed for the right words. "Maybe he *was* different before he went to prison."

Through the open window, the scent of pine and fresh air drifted into the Jeep, a welcome antidote to a memory of the cloying smells of stale tobacco and alcohol that had lingered in the house. "I don't think so. She once told me that he was charming when he wanted to be. I guess she fell for it and got pregnant. When I was a kid, my grandfather said he loaded his shotgun and went after him. He always hated my father.''

"I remember your grandfather. He was nice." Fondly she thought of the gray-haired man who'd owned a barbershop, who used to play Santa Claus at the community center at Christmastime. Jake looked like his father, but Leigh had always believed he'd taken after his mother's family. Gentle, hard-working people, they'd been a strong part of the community. Rykers had always been outcasts.

"As promised." He braked in front of the diner and glanced askance at her. Almost tauntingly, the morning sun's light shone golden strands among coppery ones. "You're on time."

Barely, Leigh noted with a glance at the dashboard clock. "I have to hurry." For his sake, she wished she could give him more time, but maybe it was best she couldn't.

Too close. They were getting too close.

In unison with him, she slammed her door. It was then she saw a scowling Al blocking the entrance to the diner.

"I need to talk to you," he said to Jake. Hesitancy flickered in his eyes. "Leigh, whatever you hear, don't tell anyone. Okay?"

Curiosity piqued, Leigh planted her feet. "I'm not even a second cousin to Grace," she said to reassure him.

Al mustered up a ghost of a smile. "I know that. Hell, I remember her cousin—what was her name?"

"Lily."

He rolled the name off his tongue slowly. "Lily. That's right."

Impatience tugged at Jake. He'd been gone long enough to be out of step with the snail's pace of Pineview. "Is there news about Seaton?" he asked, interrupting before they began listing Grace's family tree.

"Yeah." Al craned his neck and glanced around as if worried about privacy. "They had an all-points bulletin out for the truck they thought Seaton had stolen," he said in a low voice. "It was found. He abandoned it, so they figure he's still somewhere in the woods outside of town."

Why hadn't he gone somewhere else? Leigh wondered. Why had his destination been Pineview? An image returned of him in handcuffs, screaming at her that he'd get even as he was led from the courthouse.

"And the town council's upset," Al grumbled. "The FBI thinks we're bungling hicks because we don't have a sheriff."

"The FBI usually comes in like gangbusters," Jake assured him.

"Yeah, well..." Al hesitated, then motioned with his head toward a black van, a monstrosity parked in front of the sheriff's office. "That's the task force's command center. I've been in there three times to get information. They give me zilch. Bits and pieces of their plans. I thought a big-city cop would get more attention. The head guy's name is Hamil. Would you go in and talk to them?"

Jake held out a hand, palm up. "I don't have any authority here, Al."

"No, but you can show your credentials. They might carry more weight than my deputy's badge does. Would you? Eddie and me, we need some answers, or neither of us will have a job before the week ends."

Leigh didn't need to hear more. Jake would help. Her father had once told her that no matter where he went he was always a cop. Not wanting to hear Jake's response, she stepped around Al and into the diner.

If she thought she could escape Jake inside, she was wrong. He was the hot topic. Everyone seemed amazed a Ryker was one of the good guys now.

"They're talking about you and him, too," Kathleen said to her when they stood side by side in the narrow aisle behind the counter.

Leigh scooped butter into a small container and added an orange slice and parsley to a plate. "Nothing's happening."

"You're seeing him."

"As a friend."

Kathleen gave an unladylike snort.

"What?" Leigh said indignantly.

"Friends?"

Friends were all they could be now, Leigh vowed. Too easily he could tilt her world and shake every certainty in her life if she gave in to the emotion—old and new—churning inside her for him. That would be a mistake, the biggest she could make. "Yes, friends."

"And did you and this friend talk about old times?"

Leigh shook her head and turned to dump grounds from the coffee brewer.

Plates in her hands, Kathleen said close to her ear, "You need to talk to him."

Leigh knew she was right. But it wasn't easy to share a secret she'd thought would never need explaining.

Hamil proved as tight-lipped as Jake had expected, but he passed on enough information to satisfy Al. Hungry, Jake wandered up to a counter stool and ordered eggs and bacon.

Busy busing tables, Leigh didn't pass by until he was nearly finished. Without asking, she refilled his coffee cup. "Did you find out anything for Al?"

"A little," he mumbled between bites of toast. "Your sister looks happy."

Her gaze roamed to Kathleen. "She deserves a fresh start."

Didn't they, too? he wanted to ask. Visually he followed Kathleen's movement from one table to another and wondered why any man wouldn't count his blessings to have her. "What happened with the ex?"

"He abandoned her and the kids because he wanted more excitement in his life."

Jake remained quiet, sensing her need to air old resentment about her sister's problems.

"How much excitement would a crop-duster pilot need?" she asked with a tinge of bafflement.

Without humor, his lips curved into a wry grin. "That's what he was?"

"Uh-huh." She'd always believed that, along with wanderlust, Kathleen's ex had had a roving eye. "And Kathleen had hated traveling around the country with him. She'd wanted security, wanted to stay here and raise her kids."

"They couldn't compromise?"

His question surprised her. "Years ago, *you'd* never have compromised about anything."

"Yes, I did. I always gave in."

"No, *I* did," she countered.

The banter came as easily as before. "Did you think I wanted to go to Grace's folly?"

Leigh bit back a smile at the reminder about the Newells' annual open house, a pretense for everyone to rave about Grace's roses.

"Loved those watercress sandwiches."

"Probably about as much as I enjoyed Friday-night demolition derby."

"You didn't enjoy that?"

Smiling, she shook her head.

"I'll be damned. I never guessed." It amazed him because there were so many little things he knew about her. He wondered if she still sat through two showings of every movie, if she still snuck a look at the back of a book to learn how a mystery ended before she began reading. "Guess that's why we hardly ever argued."

Leigh sent him an amused look. "The years have colored everything for you. We argued." Her gaze met his eyes. Eyes that were warm and deep blue, eyes that she could look at and never tire of.

She went on. "I recall a big fight we had about you going to the lake with some buddies to water-ski." The scraping of a chair drew her attention to a customer leaving. When she swung a look back at him, humor danced in his eyes.

"If I remember right, you had to work that day."

"Yes."

"But you weren't ticked because I was going water-skiing without you," he said with certainty.

She arched a brow. "Oh, wasn't I?"

He gave her a cocky grin. "You were mad because Tim Statler's sister was going with us and she had the hots for me."

Leigh tsked. "What an ego."

"Truth hurts."

Peripherally she saw the cook slide an order on the counter. "I wasn't jealous."

He kept grinning.

"I wasn't." Leigh swung around and balanced one plate on her forearm and wedged another in the cup of her palm. "Only a little," she muttered in passing, smiling as she heard his pleased laugh behind her. Leigh wove a path around tables to deliver the order—Denver omelet and a Belgian waffle ladened with whipped cream—to the two women in a corner booth.

Candice Moore practically drooled over her waffle for a second, but only a second. "He seems different." The inquisitive look in her eyes contradicted her feigned blasé expression. "Is he?"

"Why don't you talk to him and find out for yourself?"

"Well, you knew him best. After all, you two were together all the time before he—he left."

Dumped me, is what she really meant, Leigh surmised, retracing her steps. In response to Jake digging his wallet from his back pocket, she paused at the register.

"Al said they still have a dance every weekend. How about going tonight?"

She kept her eyes on the slots in the drawer. "I can't."

"Come on," he said lightly, aware if he tried to steamroll her, she'd go toe-to-toe with him. "Take a chance."

That brought her head up. He didn't play fair. If he did, he wouldn't have used those words, words he'd always said to cajole her into something like tubing down the river or climbing the mountain to Emerald Lake and skiing down it, words that reminded her of the fun and the laughter they'd shared.

"Don't you want to make the gossips happy?"

"We're past the age of dating. Kids date. Grownups..." She wasn't sure what adults called being together these days. She hadn't been out with any man since Ken except Mark. And every time with him had been a chance meeting. She'd never accepted his offers for dinner or a movie, because she was out of practice, because she hadn't wanted to go through the hassle again.

"I'm waiting. What do you call it?"

"Are you laughing at me?"

"*With* you," he returned quickly, then took a different approach. "You're going, aren't you?"

"I'm going," she said, not bothering to clarify that she planned to go alone.

"With someone else?"

Leigh nearly smiled.

"That guy Mark?"

"He's a friend," she said cautiously, reaching for his money.

"A friend?"

His fingertips grazed her knuckles during the exchange. The contact was brief, but not brief enough. Her muscles tensed, warning her that a battle had begun.

"What do you call it when *he* asks you out?"

"We don't go out."

Not liking the sound of that, he inclined his head to see her face. "He just comes over?"

"No, he . . ." Leigh drew a stabilizing breath, an exasperated one. How had this started? "I see him occasionally," she said, handing Jake change.

"So he's only an acquaintance."

"A friend. Like Doc Higley's a friend."

"Come on, Leigh. Doc Higley's sixty-three years old. Wendley's in his thirties."

"Just what is the point to this conversation?"

God, he'd missed that flustered tone of hers. "I'm trying to find out if there's competition."

"There's no competition."

He shot an amused smile at her. "That's reassuring."

Leigh sighed that he'd sneakily gotten that admission out of her. "That's not what I meant, and you

know it. We're strictly friends now, Jake. There can't
be—"

"We'll always be friends," he cut in, sensing she was
about to say something he didn't want to hear. Leaning forward, he placed a wispy kiss on her eyebrow.
And they'd always be more than friends. "I'll pick
you up at seven," he added, and stepped away before
she could refuse.

Chapter Six

Just like that. *I'll pick you up at seven.*

All afternoon, Leigh tried to work up indignation and failed. By break time, she needed quiet more than anything else and headed for the gazebo at the center of town.

Passing her favorite dress shop, she slipped into it, intending only to browse. A white summery dress with tiny blue flowers waved at her.

Ten minutes later, she left the shop, dangling a bag, and spent the walk back to the diner convincing herself that she hadn't bought the dress for him.

In a fitful mood, she scurried into the diner and shoved the bag under the counter. Maybe she'd return the dress. Maybe she'd wear the dowdiest one in her closet.

* * *

By six-thirty that evening, Jake was watching the clock. It annoyed him that, like an adolescent whose hormones were in overdrive, he was counting the minutes until he picked her up.

With half an hour to spare, he was dressed and ready to leave, except for his shoes. He punched out his partner's phone number.

His new baby howling in the background, Bob yelled, "How's life in the hicks?"

"Haven't seen a mugging."

"Did you learn anything?"

Jake reached for his wristwatch on the table beside the bed. "No one's too cooperative."

"Did you see her?"

Cradling the receiver between his jaw and shoulder, Jake fastened the watch. "I've seen her."

"Old and ugly?"

More beautiful than ever. "She's the same," he said, scanning the beige carpet for his shoes.

"And her old man?"

Swiftly he summarized the past days.

"No husband. Unhappy about you being a cop. Wary." Bob listed reasons as if he were counting from one to three. "Doesn't sound encouraging."

If he had an ounce of good sense he'd go home and forget about the fire report, and about what used to be between Leigh and him. Then again, he'd never been too sensible where she was concerned. Years ago, he'd been willing to battle the whole damn town to be with her. Ironically, the only one standing in their way now was her.

Though he understood the fear she'd developed toward his work, he'd faced worse opposition. Whether she liked it or not, he didn't plan to fade quietly out of her life.

In her house, Leigh lounged in a tub of warm water. She'd had a notion that a relaxing bath would help. It wasn't. She was as nervous as the first time she'd dated him. Minutes later, she shimmied into her new dress, a white sleeveless with a scooped neckline, then spent more time than usual on her makeup and even polished her nails.

When the doorbell rang, she gulped down two aspirin to combat the vague pounding at her temples that signaled the start of a stress headache.

The more time she spent with him, the easier it was to erase years, but she knew better. A second time around with him meant being involved with a cop. She'd be crazy to invite disaster into her life again.

Then she opened the door, and all she felt was a rush of pleasure.

"I thought of bringing you flowers or candy."

She was relieved he hadn't. On top of the resurgence of too many emotions, the last thing she needed was to be romanced. "You did once."

Sliding a hand from her back to her waist, he looked puzzled. "No, I didn't."

Leigh smiled up at him as he guided her out the door. "Yes, you did. You picked flowers from my father's garden."

Jake arched a mocking brow. "What class!"

She shared a laugh with him over that moment, but she could have told him that she'd been delighted with those flowers. His money tight, he hadn't been able to afford too much. He'd already promised dinner and a movie. She hadn't cared where he'd gotten the flowers. She'd been thrilled by the romantic gesture. While she'd been holding the flowers, her father had strolled in scratching his head and mumbling about all his white daisies being gone.

"Guess I should tell you why I didn't bring any tonight?"

Leigh strolled with him down the porch steps. "I can hardly wait to hear."

The amusement in her voice warmed him. "I tried to get into your head and realized you'd view any gift as too romantic from a friend. So we'll wait."

His agreement to her terms of being strictly friends seemed to be coming too easy. As he opened the car door for her, Leigh slanted a look at him, nervous. "Wait for what?"

"When the time is right, I'll bring you some," he said, slamming the door before she could deliver a retort.

The moment they entered the hall of the community center, a buzz of conversation rose above the slow ballad the combo was playing. She could have avoided this moment, she knew. She should have refused to go with him. Then, she wouldn't be standing beside him now and facing curious stares with the same defiance she'd felt years ago.

Because she heard the whispers and hated them as much now as she had then, she hooked her arm in his. Because she noticed her aunt's glare, she wanted to shield him from everything. Sitting in a corner, Grace Newell's mouth flapped away. Nearby, Mark lounged against a wall, sulking. And even Kathleen wasn't beaming. "It seems we've made a grand entrance."

Jake traced her stare, then led her onto the dance floor. "Isn't this our song?" he asked to distract her from others.

Laughter bubbled in her throat. He'd always known how to handle testy moments. He'd once told her it came from lots of practice. "We never had a song."

"Let's make this one ours, then," he said about a revived old-time favorite by Nat King Cole.

As she stepped into his arms and the narrow space between them closed, it was as though they'd never been apart.

With his thumb, he stroked almost soothingly at the top of her hand. "Forget them."

She was a creature of touch, aware of his mouth smiling against her cheek, of their bodies blending against one another with their gentle swaying motion. It was crazy. She knew he'd leave again. But as her cheek rested against his, as she listened to the notes of a love song and allowed the soft music to lull her, as one dance became two, then three, Leigh faced one fact. She hadn't been alive—really alive—since he'd left, until now.

"Sleeping?" he teased, enjoying a moment much like others they'd once shared.

"You'll never let me live that down, will you?"

"I've never known anyone except you who could fall asleep while dancing."

Leigh managed her best indignant look. "I cat-napped."

"You snored."

"I did not."

"Yes, you did," he lied.

She sought a face-saving excuse. "I was tired. I'd worked all day at the diner and then helped serve a Christmas dinner at the nursing home."

With the slightest pressure at her back, he drew her closer. Having her in his arms again seemed almost unreal after years of fantasizing about such a moment. "If you remember, I wanted to skip the dance."

"Oh, but I couldn't. I'd bought that wonderful new dress."

The blue velvet. He remembered the fabric's texture, remembered how he'd thought that her skin was even softer. "Do they still have a big Christmas bash?"

"Any excuse to celebrate." Leigh moved her hand to the back of his neck. "They'll probably have one when Seaton is caught just to alleviate summertime boredom."

With her head tilted back, and her eyes, dark and sparkling, meeting his, he could almost believe there'd been no pain, no heartache, no anger.

"Did you learn any more about Seaton?"

It took effort to concentrate. Daydreaming wasn't the norm for him. He was used to staying alert even when dead tired. "Hamil's tight-lipped, but one of his men wasn't. Seaton broke into the cabin of some guy named Kahler. Authorities are trying to contact Kahler to come up here so they'll know what's missing— guns, ammunition, vehicles. . . ." His voice trailed off as her face paled. "What is it?"

"Nothing."

"Hell. Whenever something was really wrong, you'd always say it was nothing."

Leigh sighed. How well they knew each other. If she didn't give him a good answer, he'd probe relentlessly. She imagined that trait made him a tough cop.

"Give," he insisted. "Why does that news upset you?"

"That cabin is near my home."

The smile she offered to him wasn't convincing. Not all of her smiles carried the same message. This wasn't the warm one that touched her eyes. "I wouldn't worry. There are a lot of men looking for him."

As much as Leigh wanted to take his words to heart, her logic argued differently. Seaton was familiar with the terrain, he could elude them, he could get to her. "He won't be easy to find," she said instead. "Often, after a trip for weeks in the primitive area, he'd swagger into the diner to brag about his survival training."

"He'll make a mistake."

"You're sure?" she asked in a lighter tone to relax herself.

"Positive. Everyone makes a mistake sometime." He'd made a whopper the day he'd let her go, let someone else take the place in her life he'd wanted.

Over Jake's shoulder, Leigh noticed Mark weaving his way around dancing couples to reach them. Years ago, Jake had refused to give up even one dance to Gordon Howlet at the senior prom. "Remember Gordon Howlet?"

Jake drew back with a frown, wondering why she'd mentioned the muscle-bound idiot. Then he saw Wendley. In no mood for sharing her, he briefly considered knocking Wendley around. Just as quickly as the idea formed, he discarded it. His playing a jealous lover would embarrass her and make an ass out of himself. "I remember him," he answered. "He didn't have the brains to know you were mine. Still are." Lightly he brushed his lips across hers. He wanted to deepen the kiss. Instead, he stepped back and relinquished his hold on her to the man tapping him on the shoulder.

Sliding into Mark's arms, Leigh heard the music and his questioning voice, but she was breathing hard, dealing with the certainty she'd heard in Jake's words, as firm as the look she'd seen in his eyes.

"It's always been him, hasn't it?" Mark questioned.

"I can't answer that," she said honestly. "I don't know what I feel."

"But you know what you feel for me."

This wasn't any easier than she'd expected. "I've tried to be fair to you."

"You have been." He gave her hand a gentle squeeze. "It might be wise not to forget, though, that he hurt you, that he left. If he did it before, he'll do it again, Leigh." Genuine worry marked his tone. "He's not the kind of man you want in your life."

If only she didn't, but she'd never loved anyone other than Jake. No, that wasn't true—she didn't still love him. He stormed her senses whenever he touched her. But that was desire, not love, she tried to convince herself.

At the last notes of the song, she stepped from the dance floor with Mark. A glance around the room for Kathleen was a mistake. Her eyes locked with Grace's. Trapped, she politely listened to the woman's ideas for cultural activities at next year's Founder's Day celebration. Leigh inched backward. Silently she thanked Louisa Melbourne, who joined in. While the two debated about a concert or an art fair, Leigh slipped away, keeping to herself that she favored the annual softball game.

She worked her way past neighbors and friends to the makeshift bar where Al was talking to Jake. She hadn't made it her destination because of him, she assured herself. It made sense she'd want to know if Al had more news about Seaton.

"The town's being converged on," Al was telling
Jake when she sidled close. "Fifty people have joined
in the search according to Lester Newell, who's passing on what he's learned from the town's most reli-
able source—his wife." Al eyed the beer in Jake's
hand and sipped his coffee. "I don't know who's
running the operation. The people from the forest
service, sheriff's department, border patrol and state
Department of Corrections are all bumping into one
another. They're even bringing in trackers and bloodhounds from the state prison."

Feeling Leigh tense beside him, Jake curbed an im-
pulse to gather her close. As a cop, he was prone to
protective instincts, but he'd never been so on edge
before. The more he heard about Seaton, the more he
didn't want to let Leigh out of his sight.

"So what do you think?" Al asked, staring at Jake
as if he should have answers.

He wished he did. He wished he knew why she
hadn't waited. He wished he could understand why
two people meant for each other had lost ten years.
Listening to Al, he looked past him to the woman sitting in the corner. She was watching him like an eagle
ready to swoop down on its prey. Abigail Martin
would never be one of his favorite people. To what
extent had she been responsible for everything that had
gone wrong between him and Leigh?

"Eddie and I aren't sure how to handle this," Al
said, cutting into Jake's thoughts.

"If you want, I'll stop at the office tomorrow, and
we'll talk."

"Man, me and Eddie can use any help we can get."

Help? Jake stifled a laugh. It seemed strange, being in Pineview and having anyone ask him for help.

"Will you help them?" Leigh questioned as they wandered toward the buffet table.

He cast a quick look at Wendley. "I don't know about them, but I was ready to rescue you."

She caught his glare at Mark and reached for a cookie. "Were you?"

The teasing tone was so familiar he felt his heart twist. She'd always been light-spirited, almost impish, despite a serious, practical nature. He'd loved that airiness in her. Hell, he'd loved everything about her. "Having fun at my expense?" he asked good-naturedly.

Leigh laughed. "A little."

"I'm glad someone's having a good time tonight," a voice said behind them.

Marvin Tebner, the mayor, cozied up to them. During Jake's senior year, Tebner had been his history teacher. He was gray now, balding with a neat salt-and-pepper beard and wire-rimmed glasses, and he still liked the sound of his own voice. Tebner was at his best.

"Everyone's so keyed up about Seaton that they want me to deputize all of them. And tourism is down and will stay that way as long as Seaton's haunting the woods around here."

"Can't be too bad," Jake quipped, surveying the buffet table. "All the motels are filled with FBI agents and reporters."

Tebner's dull mood brightened, stirring his smile and a crinkling of lines at the corners of his eyes. "You always simplified everything," he said with a chuckle. He gave Jake a hopeful look. "You liked history, didn't you? Admit it now."

Jake noticed Grace Newell's brownies still looked rock hard. "And ruin my reputation?"

The older man gave another laugh. "I always liked having you in my class."

He could have fooled Jake.

Nibbling on a cracker, Leigh shared an amused smile with him, but peripherally she saw Kathleen and Jim in a corner. Her sister's agitated gestures declared trouble.

"Do you remember that you challenged everything from Columbus discovering America to Paul Revere's warning cry?" Tebner went on, not expecting an answer. "Other teachers viewed you as a troublemaker. I thought you were more inquisitive than the rest in my class." He scanned the crowded room in the manner of a king looking over his subjects. "I bet you're an excellent policeman."

Painfully Leigh had come to the same conclusion. Jake was made of the right fiber to be in law enforcement. Honest, obstinate and relentless. Cops like that never stopped pursuing or putting themselves in danger. For a little while on the dance floor, the clock had turned back. It had all seemed so natural, so right, that she'd nearly forgotten the one reason she'd never allow him back in her life.

"He's gone. You can talk now," Jake urged because she'd been so quiet.

She presented a smile, resolving to keep her thoughts, as well as her feelings, to herself.

With Jake's gentle nudge, Leigh traced his stare to Marvin scurrying toward the microphone. "The mayor's about to give a speech. I suppose it's too soon to leave?" Jake asked quietly.

"Actually, it's the perfect time."

In silence, they drove through town. A warm breeze blew through the Jeep. In minutes, she'd be home, safe from needs and wants. She didn't care that she was running from him. Running might be her only defense.

She turned her face to the wind, letting it whip through her hair. They wouldn't do this again. No soft words or stirring sensations could eclipse the sadness a life with him might bring into a woman's heart.

Ending her distracted gaze at the trees whizzing by, she looked forward. Moonlight shimmered on the lake, dappling pines and aspens with light. And, as if cast in a spotlight, a patch of wildflowers still peeked from behind a rock at the edge of the forest.

Déjà vu slipped over her. For a long moment, she stared at a clearing that was a few feet back from the lake where spruce and pine surrounded one giant willow, where they'd sat in a secondhand car he'd borrowed. Night after night, he'd drawn her into his dream to build a house there—their house. For hours, they'd talked and visualized the rooms.

Leigh dragged her eyes away from the willow, from a memory of hot kisses, relentless hands, gasping breaths. An ache, quick and sharp, whipped through her. Lost dreams filled her mind. It wasn't supposed to have happened this way. How many times had she thought that? For a moment, she closed her eyes, overwhelmed by how much they'd really lost.

Jake merely glanced at the place they'd built their dreams on. She'd had dreams with another man, he was forced to remember. Where? Where had she lived with Grentham? He didn't really want to know details. There'd be too much fury, too much hurt, if he learned too much. "Grentham filled the vacancy left by Jed Ehber, didn't he?"

The mention of Ken came so unexpectedly it took Leigh a moment to find her voice. "Yes, he retired about a month before you left," she answered, uneasy that he might ask more questions. There were some she didn't want to answer, didn't know how to. If possible, she'd have explained why she'd married Ken, but could he understand her vulnerability without knowing everything? "Ken and my father got along well. It was as if Ken was the son he never had. Because he was always around the house, I saw a lot of him."

Jake had disliked Grentham for a lot of reasons. A few years older than him and sporting a badge, Grentham had announced to Jake that Leigh McCall was his. Jake had met those words with a laugh. He was the one who held her, who made love to her, not Grentham. In the end, Grentham had had the last laugh. "Must have been a whirlwind romance. You married him within a couple of months after I left, didn't you?"

What could she say? *You weren't here. I needed someone.* "It was too quick," she admitted, glad he was driving and his eyes were fixed on the road instead of her. "Our marriage wasn't everything I'd hoped for. It just happened."

Old resentments close at hand, Jake let silence build between them as he turned onto her street. It wasn't difficult to imagine her father's brainwashing against him. "So you married him on the rebound?"

"You make it sound so simple." Dark and intense, his stare probed as if to see inside her. She didn't want him to see too much. "You still have a tendency to look at everything as black and white."

"Cops do. Your father was the same way. In his mind, I couldn't be good for you. I was a Ryker." He braked in front of her house and let the engine idle. "So after I left—" he snapped his fingers "—you just fell in love with someone else."

At that moment, she wished for the strength to strangle him. Did he really think she could switch that emotion from one man to another so easily? "I didn't think you'd come back."

Something slammed at him as if he'd been punched in the stomach. "What did you want from me?" He couldn't keep the irritation out of his voice. This wasn't the way he'd wanted the evening to go, but he had no control left. He'd checked his temper but couldn't dodge the hurt. "After I wrote to you, and you didn't answer the letter, that's when I called my father, that's when I learned you were married.''

Leigh simply stared at him in the dark car, his words echoing in her brain. "You wrote to me?" All this time, she'd thought, she'd agonized, believing he'd walked away and had never looked back.

Peering at her, Jake leaned closer and saw the truth in her eyes. "You never got the letter?"

"No," she whispered the word. Her eyes closed. She wanted to cry. *A letter*. One word from him and she'd have waited.

He pressed back against the seat as anger surfaced in him so quickly it nearly rocked him. "Damn him."

"Maybe..." Leigh wrestled with bewilderment. Her father wouldn't have deliberately kept that letter from her. "Maybe it never got here. Maybe—"

"Maybe it came and he threw it away."

"He'd never do that. It couldn't have gotten here," she insisted with a small shake of her head. Her father wouldn't have done that to her. He'd loved and cared and tried to console her.

She'd been sitting in her room, staring at photos of her and Jake when her father had come in. He'd been so understanding, so sympathetic. She'd cried in his arms about Jake being gone, and he'd soothed her. She had her whole life ahead of her, he'd said. She needed to get out. Her heart aching, she hadn't wanted to go anywhere, but at his urging, she'd joined him at the dinner table. Ken had been there.

During the next two weeks he'd had dinner with them every night. She hadn't been thinking straight then, and as weeks passed, she'd bowed to her father's opinion—Jake would never come back.

She knew her father had always believed that Jake, being a Ryker, would bring her nothing but unhappiness. Possibly her father had taken the letter to protect her from more heartache, believing if she'd mattered so much to Jake, he'd never have left her. "If you had said goodbye—"

He heard the accusation and hurt threading her voice. "I couldn't."

"Why couldn't you?" she asked, needing to understand.

Didn't she realize how much he'd loved her? She'd made the air worth breathing, had given him purpose and direction. She'd been the only person who'd ever really loved him. "There was a lot going on. I couldn't. I had my reasons."

Reasons he wouldn't share with her. That was best. If they healed wounds, he could inflict another on her. "It doesn't really matter anymore, does it?"

"It still matters," he said softly. "If it doesn't, then why did you come with me tonight?"

More than anything, she wished for a moment alone to think clearly. He'd never grant her even a second. "To prove something to both of us," she said, knowing he'd never let her leave the Jeep without some response.

"Prove what?"

"Prove to myself that it's over."

"Is it?" he asked in a tone harsher than he'd intended, but he wondered how she could even utter those words when his gut tightened just from the sound of her voice. "Let's really prove it.".

Suddenly trapped by his arm, Leigh drew back. "There's nothing to prove," she said, breathless as his hand weaved into her hair and his face leaned closer. She knew her protest was useless as his mouth closed over hers.

Dark and disturbing sensations shot through her. She trembled beneath the hunger she felt in the lips on hers. For years, she'd convinced herself that she'd forgotten him, that he was part of her past. She knew now she'd been an idiot to believe that. Needs mushroomed within her.

Straining against him, she curled her arms around his back, meeting the demand of his mouth, the urgency, wanting the closeness. Heady with the pleasure, she savored the familiar, marveled in the change.

Her heart hammered, echoing a message she couldn't ignore. She sought his taste, his tongue, the warm recesses of his mouth. And she ached for more. She had no more than another second, she realized. If she didn't stop, she'd be his.

One yesterday long ago, she'd have given him her very soul. But this was now, and he was different. The amalgam of grief and loneliness and confusion she'd endured taunted her to remember that years ago she'd grieved for him as surely as if he'd died. And he'd left, not caring if she was all right. "No more." Before she couldn't, she bounded from the car.

She reminded herself over and over—if he'd loved her, he wouldn't have left.

* * *

Jake watched the door close behind her and swore softly. So much was unsaid, unexplained, but all of the unanswered questions didn't matter. There was no one but her—the taste of her, the scent that reminded him of springtime. Insatiable wanting had clawed at him. He'd wanted to take her, feel her softness, drown in her sweetness. He'd wanted to feel the slender curves that had rounded to a woman's body, but she had to come to him willingly. It wasn't the frenzy whenever they kissed that he wanted. He longed for more—her love. And he knew this time would be different.

This time he wouldn't leave without her.

Chapter Seven

Jake eyed the clock on the wall of the sheriff's office. Al was slouched back in his chair, yawning, his hands folded over a paunch. "'Morning. You got good timing, Jake."

Eddie whistled as he came through the door behind Jake and skirted around him to plop down the carton in his hands.

As he flipped it open to reveal a variety of iced doughnuts, Al came to attention in his chair. "Sure do like these. Want one?"

Jake surveyed the feast of cholesterol-laden goodies and shook his head.

Eddie's brows lowered. "You one of those health nuts?"

"Depends on what you consider healthy."

"Granola bars and them funny sprouts that the mayor has on his salads all the time," Eddie piped in.

Settling on the chair across from Al, Jake fished into his shirt pocket for a cigarette. "Sounds too healthy," he said, putting to rest rumors of his being a health fanatic once and for all. "Did you talk to the town council?"

"I talked to the mayor." Al selected a chocolate doughnut. "Love these with the sprinkles on 'em. The mayor said he told them what you wanted." Al offered an apologetic look. "I'm sorry. They said no."

"Abby Martin did," Jake said with certainty.

Al finished chewing. "That's a good guess. I'd like to help you, but I can't. I'll lose my job, Jake, if I give you the keys to the file storage room. I can't afford to do that. I got a wife and two kids." He shot an annoyed look at the ringing phone, then reached for it.

Jake circled the room visually. He'd been in it a few times while growing up, hauled in for pranks that he realized now had given Leigh's father his share of headaches.

The squeak of Al's chair swung him around.

Al snatched up handcuffs from a desk drawer and stood. "We got to go, Eddie. Seaton's been spotted again, out at the canyon. A police helicopter is trying to stay with him. Everyone's been called to go out there. You coming?" he asked, nudging Jake in passing.

Besides having no business nosing into this case, he couldn't think of a good reason why he should bother. The town had never done a damn thing for him. But he was a cop. It was an occupation that didn't differentiate between time on or off the clock.

Out of sync. Leigh hadn't gotten into a natural rhythm since she'd awakened. She'd dumped half of the old coffee grounds from the brewer onto the floor instead of into the garbage can, she'd bumped her toe into the leg of her vanity table so savagely that she'd rocked for several seconds in pain, and she'd capped off her morning by dropping her hairbrush in the toilet.

Sitting at the kitchen table and nursing a cup of coffee, she waited for Kathleen's arrival. She wondered now if she should renege on a promise to go bike riding. She'd probably fall off and skin her knee like a ten-year-old.

It was all Jake's fault. She'd gone beyond responding last night. She'd been urging him, craving. She'd been thinking about nothing but him, not even where she was. She'd been wrapped up in him, in his mouth on hers and the warmth of his body. She'd wanted him again. Maybe she had never stopped wanting only him.

She closed her eyes and tried to blot out all her thoughts. It didn't work. If she wasn't reflecting about Jake, she was thinking about her father. She'd believed in him, in his goodness, and her heart suddenly weighed heavy with doubts.

Efforts to rationalize what she knew only left her with more questions. Why did her father think Leonard Ryker was guilty of that fire if he knew Jake's father had had an alibi? And *had* he prevented her from seeing the letter from Jake? Leigh gnawed at her thumbnail, not sure she wanted answers to those questions.

At the sound of a car engine, she roused herself. Flicking off the dial on the radio, she halted Garth Brooks in midnote, then ambled outside.

While she wheeled her ten-speed out of the storage shed, Kathleen unloaded her own bike from the rack on the back of her Bronco. Over her shoulder, Kathleen studied her for a long moment. "You look lousy."

"Thank you."

"Didn't you sleep well?" Kathleen asked with what sounded like sisterly concern.

Leigh chose the least personal of her worries as a handy excuse. "I kept wondering about Seaton."

Kathleen reached across and blocked her from mounting her bike. "Who's really bothering you? Seaton or Jake?"

Leigh decided never to aspire to an acting job. "I thought Seaton would be in Montana or Canada by now," she answered to sidestep her sister's perception.

"I thought he'd be caught by now."

Neither had happened. He was somewhere in the woods near her home. Too close. Much too close.

"You're a lot more worried than you're letting on, aren't you?"

"Yes. Want to know why?"

Kathleen paused in fastening her helmet, and in big-sister fashion, she gave Leigh her full attention.

"I'm worried we're going to get soaked before we get back," Leigh said, sweeping an arm toward the sky, which was graying with heavy clouds and promising a summer storm.

"I thought you were going to say something interesting." Kathleen glanced upward. "It won't rain until tonight."

Leigh loved her sister's optimism. She absolutely refused to let anything drag down her spirits. Leigh knew her methods for weathering troubled times. Since her divorce, Kathleen had tried her hand at a lot of odd projects, from polishing rocks to growing cacti for sale. Busywork, Leigh assumed, to keep from dwelling on a jerk of an ex-husband. "Is that wishful thinking or are you into predicting weather now?"

Kathleen took her teasing in stride. "I listened to the weather report this morning. No thunderstorms until tonight. Ready?" she asked as they mounted their bikes.

"You lead."

Kathleen took off. "Top of the hill before the Material Girl finishes her song."

Leigh pumped hard, trailing her and the blaring radio. As they coasted down, she looked to see if Kathleen was huffing as hard as she was. Not on a bet. It amazed her that a woman three years older, with two children, was in better shape. "Slow down."

Hunching forward, Kathleen downed the volume on the radio. "Getting old?"

"No, I am not. But I want to talk." *And breathe.* "Did you and Jim decide on a date yet?"

"He's been busy. His friend Dale arrived last night."

Clearly Kathleen wasn't pleased. "That's nice for Jim," Leigh said.

Kathleen gave her an everything-is-not-okay smile.

Leigh slowed her pace. "You don't like Dale?"

"Yes, I like him."

"Kathleen, I saw you and Jim last night. I know trouble when I see it."

"If I told you I bought three pints of butter pecan ice cream, would that be enough of an answer?"

More than enough, Leigh thought. Kathleen had gained twenty-five pounds because of a love affair with ice cream after her ex had left. "If I reminded you how hard it was to lose the weight the last time, would you listen?"

Her sister's eyes brightened with laughter. "Have no fear. I took the ice cream, opened one carton, ate two teaspoonsful and gave the rest to my next door neighbor."

"Good."

"You're disgustingly disciplined."

"Annoying, too, huh?"

They shared a smile.

"Now, tell me the problem," Leigh insisted.

"Dale's— He's nice." She signaled to take a side road that led to the canyon. "He's an Indy driver."

"Indy? He's been in the race?"

Kathleen smoothed one errant reddish blond strand away from her face. "No, he's going to be. This is his first year. And whenever the two of them are together, that's all they talk about."

It seemed logical to Leigh that a mechanic would be engrossed in the stories of a race-car driver, but she saw that some of Kathleen's excitement about a forthcoming marriage had ebbed. "Are you feeling neglected?"

Kathleen released a short laugh. "I'm not a child who needs constant attention. But I'm concerned. Jim's wrapped up in the excitement of everything that Dale keeps telling him."

"Isn't that natural?"

"I suppose so."

"Jim's everything you want, isn't he? Stable and responsible and—"

"You don't have to sell him to me," Kathleen said lightly. "You know how I feel about him."

In response to the droning of a helicopter, Leigh tilted her head toward the sky. "Sounds like love."

"And you?"

Leigh pedaled faster. "What about me?"

"Are you involved with Jake again?"

Sneaky, Leigh mused. Though she'd prepared herself for her sister's barrage of questions, when she hadn't asked one, Leigh had begun to relax.

"Too tough a question?"

"We can't go back. No one can. You know that. It's why you've started to make a new life for yourself and the kids."

"Why can't you?"

Leigh turned her head slightly to shade her eyes from the fierce wind. "You know why I can't."

"Leigh, there are some women who love only one." She arched a brow. "Thank God, I'm not one of them. But you—"

"Love?" Leigh didn't bother to veil her disbelief. "He's been gone ten years."

"And now he's back. Why did you go to the dance with him if he means nothing to you anymore?" she asked in a tone Leigh had heard her use with her children when they'd been squabbling and she wanted the truth. "Face it, some of that past will always bind the two of you. You shared something that—"

"Kathleen, please don't," Leigh practically pleaded.

"Okay, but—" She kept whatever she'd planned to say to herself.

Ahead of them, a throng of media and a crowd of curious neighbors stood on the side of the road. To their right, gathered at the edge of the canyon, a multitude of state troopers and public-safety officers rambled around.

Leigh spotted Jake standing near Al Deavers and several highway patrol officers at a roadblock as if he were one of them. Stopping, she and Kathleen dismounted, then walked their bikes forward, toward the canyon and Jake. Leigh waited until they were near him. "Did they find Seaton?"

Her face remained calm, but her voice signaled an anxiousness that made Jake want to draw her close. He resisted the urge, knowing she'd pridefully stiffen. "He's down in the canyon."

Leigh took off her helmet. Bloodhounds, bluetick hounds and a cream-and-tan Walker sniffed along the canyon wall. They'd never find Seaton down there, was her first thought. The canyon's steep walls and rocky floor choked with shrubs would limit the search. He had hundreds of good hiding places.

Her helmet in her hand, she shook her hair. "This is the third time he's been seen somewhere around here. I wonder if he really has been or people are just imagining that someone looks like him."

"This time it was him," Jake assured her. "A Forest Service ranger spotted him and took chase. When Seaton reached the highway, he almost ran into a state trooper's car. They stopped and tried to pursue him, but he raced down the canyon. How he didn't break his neck amazes me."

"So he really is nearby." Uneasiness settled over Kathleen's face. "You could stay in town with me."

Leigh was the serious, cautious one, not Kathleen. That she'd made such a suggestion punctuated her anxiety. Leigh nudged her arm hard with an elbow. "Don't let me down now and get too maternal."

A smile, though forced, curved Kathleen's lips. "I save that for my kids."

Leigh zeroed in on Jake again. "Are you part of all this now?"

That she wasn't pleased was obvious. "As long as I'm here, I offered to help in the search."

Leigh kept her thoughts to herself about him endangering his life when he didn't have to. In a way, she understood why he'd volunteered. Inside the man remained a hint of the boy who'd left and was still trying to be a part of the town.

Because he needed to touch her, Jake brushed a strand of hair away from her cheek. "Be careful going back home."

Careful. She was always careful. She didn't speed, she wore her seat belt, she didn't leave her door unlocked. She was a disgustingly cautious person. Yet could she be watchful enough as long as Seaton wasn't caught—as long as Jake was in town?

Before she reached home, an idea had taken hold. Though unsettled over what she planned to do, she knew of only one way to ease Jake out of her life. Her own seesawing emotions demanded some kind of action quickly.

During her break that afternoon, she drove out of town, toward the huge Victorians on the hill. She wheeled into the winding driveway outside her aunt's house then hurried to the front door.

The maid, a gray-haired woman with the apparent disposition of a saint—necessary to be an employee of her aunt for nearly fifteen years—beamed and ushered her out to the garden.

A colorful array of orange, yellow and blue blossoms danced on the summer breeze. Their scent mingled with the trace of pine from the trees in the woods behind the house and the hint of rain saturating the air.

Her glasses propped on the bridge of her nose, her aunt, as always, was immaculately dressed. This morning she wore a gray linen dress with a single strand of pearls, and she looked not the least affected by the humidity.

At the click of Leigh's boots across the parquet floor, Abby looked up from the newspaper in her hand. "This is an unexpected surprise. You're not working today?"

"Yes, I am." Leigh placed a greeting kiss on her aunt's velvety cheek. "I have only a few minutes to talk."

With regal slowness, she folded the newspaper before her. Abby McCall, daughter of a hardware-store owner, had taken her position as the town's grande dame seriously ever since her marriage to Thomas Martin over thirty years ago. After his death, she'd assumed his position as the town's leader. She'd never held any public office; none had been necessary. It was expected that the mayor and town council would defer to her opinion on everything. "Would you like tea or coffee or—"

Leigh shook her head, halting her aunt's sweeping hand as it motioned to her right, toward the small buffet.

"This isn't a social call?"

"No, not really." Leigh took a seat on the wrought-iron chair opposite her. "I'd like you to okay the release of the report that Jake wants to see."

Her aunt's steely gaze met hers. "I've already made my decision. I don't plan to change it."

Here goes, Leigh mused. "I thought you might say that. I'm asking you to do this for me, not him."

"I see he's already turned your head again." She made the comment without looking up from stirring her tea.

"No, he hasn't. I came hoping you'd agree." Leigh's stomach fluttered. "He won't leave until he sees it."

"And that bothers you?"

Leigh managed a quick nod.

"I'm pleased to hear you've come to your senses about him."

Oh, but she hadn't.

"However, you don't need to be concerned about him staying. He's a Ryker. He'll be on his way soon." Leigh sent her a doubtful look that drew a vague smile to her aunt's face. "I see you don't agree with me. Well, if he's still here when I get back, we'll discuss this again."

"Back?"

"Yes, for a few days I'll be in Tucson on business and to see friends." Across the table, she patted Leigh's hand reassuringly. "He'll tire of being here. He did before, didn't he?"

Leigh couldn't argue. Perhaps she was worrying unnecessarily. Jake's abrupt departure before had proved that no one had meant enough to him to keep him in Pineview. Her aunt was right. He'd leave soon, whether he got the report or not.

By evening, as darkness descended, a storm had begun. Dodging puddles, Leigh dashed to her car from the diner. She liked rain, but not storms, sometimes violent and destructive. Peering between the swishing windshield wipers, she hoped the power stayed on through the night with Seaton so near.

Drenched by the time she ran into the house, she grabbed a towel and dried off while she sat by the bay window in the living room and watched the onslaught. Behind her, music floated from the stereo, the soothing sounds of Lorrie Morgan.

Outside, branches swayed beneath an irate wind. Fingers of lightning reached downward, brightening the room with an eerie flash. Rain pounded at the roof of the house as if trying to invade.

For several minutes, she listened to the wailing wind. Thunder rumbled, breaking up the lonely quiet surrounding her. An emptiness she hadn't acknowledged in years brewed anew. As the lights flickered, Leigh bolted to a stand and rummaged in a kitchen cupboard for candles.

Tucking matches in her jeans pocket, she pulled bread and cheese out of the refrigerator. Cooking for one offered little incentive. Behind her, the coffee brewer released a final hiss.

While she placed buttered bread in a frying pan, rain thudded harder against the roof, as if trying to bore holes through the shingles. For a long moment, she stood still and listened. Had she imagined the creaking of the porch steps or was she on edge because of the storm?

She wouldn't panic. She was a nineties woman. She could take care of herself. She sucked in a breath, wishing her knees would listen to her mind and stop shaking. For what it was worth, she reached into the cupboard for a heavy cast-iron skillet.

She tightened her fingers on the handle, but what she needed to do was stop acting like a heroine in a gothic tale and imagining things that go bump in the night. No one was out—

Leigh gasped at the shadow outside her kitchen window. Someone was definitely there, looking in, staring at her. Never letting her eyes stray from the window, she raised the skillet and scooted toward the telephone.

"Leigh?" Rain dripping down his face, Jake peered at her through the window.

In relief, she sagged back against the counter. Her heart banging against the wall of her chest, she flung open the door and greeted Jake with a drilling look. "I nearly knocked you out cold."

Amused, he eyed the skillet in her hand. "I remembered you didn't like storms."

She steeled herself, not wanting his words to touch her, but as he strolled in as if he belonged, Leigh acknowledged her weakness. If she spent too much time with him, none of those heartbreaking years would matter. "I'll get you a towel."

Jake scanned the room. It was freshly painted. She'd changed nothing. Her mother's needlepoints of Indian baskets adorned the wall over a kitchen desk. A small library of cookbooks occupied two shelves near the stove. And a wicker basket with dried wild-flowers that she'd laughingly presented to her father one Father's Day was propped in a corner.

"Here." Leigh tossed him a towel, then pivoted around to the stove to rescue the sandwiches from the pan before they burned. "It's a lousy night to be out driving."

Thoughtfully he studied her while he dragged the towel over his wet hair. "I knew where I was going."

The sureness in his voice prompted her to look up. With his face only inches from hers, desire skittered though her. Desire she didn't want to resist.

"Smells good." So did she, her fragrance enticing him to lean closer. "Always liked grilled cheese."

With an unsteady sigh, she resigned herself to the uphill battle ahead, as too many soft feelings for him seemed a breath away. "If you'd like something else, I could make—"

"The sandwich is fine." Didn't she realize he'd have given the same answer for a tuna casserole, something women found delicious and he hated? He'd have eaten anything if it meant more time with her.

At the chime of the grandfather clock in her father's study, he gave her the space he sensed she wanted and ambled to the doorway. On a hallway wall hung graduation photographs of Leigh and Kathleen. He'd always envied the warmth and welcoming she knew whenever she'd stepped into this house after a date.

Whenever he'd walked down that dirt road toward the cottage he'd shared with his father, he'd felt as if he'd been entering quicksand, and with each day that had passed, he'd sunk a little deeper. He'd been certain that eventually he'd be sucked up by the despair he'd felt. Until Leigh had come into his life. She'd been a bundle of enthusiasm. She'd been more than his lifeline; she'd been his life. "Nothing's changed."

He was wrong. As he unzipped his Windbreaker, Leigh's eyes darted to the gun in his shoulder holster. Everything had changed. He represented what she'd vowed to keep out of her life. No matter what she still felt, no matter what bitter memories they could put behind them, they couldn't be more than friends now.

Turning around, he noticed the frown clouding her eyes, the quick look away from his service revolver. It had to be one of fate's cruel jokes that the one thing that had kept him going, that had been vital to his salvation without her—his job—would make her shun whatever they could have together.

Leigh set plates on the table and turned away to pour coffee. "I've been thinking about what you said."

He'd said a lot. Some of it he was sure she hadn't wanted to hear.

"I'm going to do what I can to help you." Keeping her distance, from across the table, she slid a coffee cup toward him. "I'll convince my aunt to give an okay so you can read the report about the fire."

Jake peered at her over the rim of his cup. "Just like that?"

"Yes," she said firmly.

The first time he'd asked her out, she'd spoken in the same tone when Jake had wondered if her father would let her go out with him. She wanted to, so her father would, she'd told Jake then. She'd been as good as her word, but he wouldn't expect the same results with her aunt. "Good luck."

"Luck won't help." Leigh settled on a chair and curled her fingers around the cup. "I'll need the persuasive powers of a snake-oil salesman," she admitted in between sips of the hot coffee.

Again thunder crashed with nerve-racking harshness. Maybe it was the weather, the stormy night, the thunder and lightning—all elements for a gothic tale—but as she gazed out the window at the night rain mantling even the silhouette of her mother's rose bush at the edge of the porch, she couldn't quiet a slim trace of fear. "They haven't found Randy Seaton yet, have they?"

Jake wiped his hands on a napkin and balled it. He hesitated to tell her what he'd learned, then decided the more she knew, the more cautious she'd be. "No, he's back in the woods. The hounds caught his scent about midafternoon. How the hell he could elude them beats me. Unless someone's hiding him."

"You think someone is?" she asked, realizing for some reason she had a lot of confidence in his instincts as a cop.

"Has he got family here?"

"A sister." Leigh set down her cup. "But they always argued."

"Some families thrive that way."

Leigh knew he was thinking about his own. "Do you really think he'll come here? Everyone knows the threat he made to me. Wouldn't he assume I was being watched, protected?"

"You are." He laid a hand on top of hers. She was still as necessary to him as air. Her smile paled sunlight. Her laugh rivaled the sweetest music he'd ever heard. Dumb, poetic thoughts, he reflected. And the truth.

He'd crawl if he thought it would do any good, but only giving her the truth would help him. And he couldn't share it, aware the hurt she'd feel afterward wasn't worth it. Instead, he shared his own bewilderment over fate's cruel hand. "I don't know why everything had to go wrong for us before, but we're right for each other." His fingertips caught her chin and forced her to look at him. "You know that."

A slow-moving shiver slithered up her spine. "We aren't the same people anymore."

Fighting a need to rush her, he kept himself from touching her. All he could do was soak up the moment, memorize the smells in the room, the way the overhead light highlighted strands at the crown of her head, the look in her eyes, and he ached for what he still wanted more than anything else—a lifetime of these comfortable, easy moments with her late at night. "Tell me what you feel, not what you think," he insisted, drawing her to stand with him.

"I don't know what I feel anymore." As his mouth hovered close, her eyes fluttered shut. She wanted to go with her emotions at that moment. She ached desperately to accept the pleasure he'd arouse, but there were more obstacles now than before. "You should go."

Images from long ago returned: her face in the moonlight as she leaned closer to him, her warmth engulfing him, her whispered words of love filling him with a wanting that had promised to consume him. "One more thing first."

Leigh felt the light pressure of his hand at the small of her back. It would have been so easy to push away, to stop this, if only she wasn't dying for the feel of his arms around her again. Swaying into him, she tried to reason, even as certainty of what she didn't want abandoned her. The mouth that closed over hers demanded nothing. It gave—with its gentleness, with its warmth. She was the one who tasted with greed this time, slanting her lips, bruising them against his. The wild craving descended on her again, the need to have him overshadowing everything.

She tried to think, to reason. Sensations, vivid and familiar, bombarded her, and she yearned. God, she longed for his slick damp flesh beneath her fingers, the heat, the oneness—the madness.

She touched his cheek, running her fingertips over the stubble of his beard, inching her fingers up to caress the strands of thick, dark hair at the nape of his neck. Caution fled just as it had once before. Her arms around him, she answered the message of his kiss, responded to the moist heat of his tongue and knew she was lost. He could have her at that moment. She was too weak to fight the longing for him.

Burying his face in her hair, he held her tight a second longer. All her denials meant nothing, but he didn't want a moment on a rainy night. He wanted it all. "I still want you," he said softly against her ear. They weren't the words he'd wanted to say. But whispers of love would make her run. This time, he'd make sure neither of them would. "Always will." Forcing himself back, he stroked her hair. Silk strands, flaming beneath the light of the kitchen, curled around his fingers as if capturing his touch and beckoning him to stay. He'd never forgotten the tenderness he'd known only with her. It was burned into his memory, taunting him whenever he'd looked into the face of another woman.

It haunted him now as he released her and crossed the kitchen to open the door. Standing in the doorway, he faced the night air, letting the mist blow at him. The curtain of rain directed his thoughts to another night, one when needs mingled with love, a night when he'd known he loved her so much he'd have died for her. No, nothing had changed, he reflected, stepping into the downpour.

Alone and shaken, Leigh pressed her fingers to her lips, swollen and warm from his kiss, then rushed to the door and watched him dash to his Jeep. Almost in surrender, she slumped against the doorframe. He'd been the one who'd taught her the wonders of loving, who she'd wanted to give everything to. Neither time nor distance had switched off those feelings.

The flutter of the summer's breeze across her face drifted her back to another night.

"Meet me at the lake later" Jake had whispered as they'd lain in a meadow of wildflowers. His hand, possessive and demanding, had skimmed her breast while his mouth had twisted across hers thoroughly, desperately. She'd felt the need in both of them, the need that seemed a breath away whenever they were together, whenever he touched her. Passion had been so painful. She'd caressed his face with her hands, pressing her lips harder to his, feeling as if she couldn't get enough of him.

Beneath the moonlight, silver lights had slanted across his dark hair. A warm breeze had rustled the branches of pines, but all she'd heard was her heart thundering, her blood pounding.

"I'm tired of sneaking around" he'd murmured.

Soothingly she'd kissed the curve of his jaw, letting her hands skim the broadness of his back as he held himself poised above her. "We can't change anything."

"Yes, I can." His breath hot on her face, his eyes dark slits beneath the mantle of the night, he'd stared at her in a way that had made her believe in him, in *them*. "Away from this town, everything will be different."

She'd tensed instinctively at those dreaded words. *But what about us?* she'd wanted to ask. *What about me? I can't live without you,* she'd wanted to tell him. *I couldn't stand a day without seeing you.* "You can't leave."

"Not without you, I won't."

Her heart had promised to burst through her chest.

"Meet me at the lake later." The words had been torn from his throat as desire had overshadowed ev-

004E681

3 WAYS TO PLAY

for big CASH prizes and FREE GIFTS!

First play your "Win-A-Fortune" game
tickets to see if you qualify for up to
£600,000 IN LIFETIME INCOME

5S5SE -that's £20,000 each year for 30 years!

See inside →

WIN A CASH FORTUNE

GAME TICKET NO. **1a**

Game ticket values vary. Scratch GOLD from Big Money Wheel
to determine the potential cash value of prize you will receive
if this ticket has a prizewinning number.

YOUR EXCLUSIVE
LUCKY NUMBER IS **BZ586811**

DO *NOT* SEPARATE - KEEP ALL TICKETS INTACT

WIN A CASH FORTUNE

GAME TICKET NO. **1b**

Game ticket values vary. Scratch GOLD from Big Money Wheel
to determine the potential cash value of prize you will receive
if this ticket has a prizewinning number.

YOUR EXCLUSIVE
LUCKY NUMBER IS **DK584100**

DO *NOT* SEPARATE - KEEP ALL TICKETS INTACT

WIN A CASH FORTUNE

GAME TICKET NO. **1c**

Game ticket values vary. Scratch GOLD from Big Money Wheel
to determine the potential cash value of prize you will receive
if this ticket has a prizewinning number.

YOUR EXCLUSIVE
LUCKY NUMBER IS **NB597296**

DO *NOT* SEPARATE - KEEP ALL TICKETS INTACT

WIN A CASH FORTUNE

GAME TICKET NO. **1d**

Game ticket values vary. Scratch GOLD from Big Money Wheel
to determine the potential cash value of prize you will receive
if this ticket has a prizewinning number.

YOUR EXCLUSIVE
LUCKY NUMBER IS **PX590204**

DO *NOT* SEPARATE - KEEP ALL TICKETS INTACT

WIN A CASH FORTUNE

GAME TICKET NO. **1e**

Game ticket values vary. Scratch GOLD from Big Money Wheel
to determine the potential cash value of prize you will receive
if this ticket has a prizewinning number.

YOUR EXCLUSIVE
LUCKY NUMBER IS **VE595496**

DO *NOT* SEPARATE - KEEP ALL TICKETS INTACT

erything again. "I love you. I'll always love you" he'd whispered.

Leigh closed her eyes to banish the memory. She waited until she could breathe and not feel the tightness in her throat, then shut the door. One thought lingered. She was opening her heart to him again.

Chapter Eight

At five the next morning, oppressive warmth smothered any breeze. In the distance, heavy clouds hung low in the predawn light and rolled slowly to the north.

Head bent, Leigh dug her car keys from her purse, anticipating the coolness of the air conditioner. She was a step from her car when she saw him. He was slouched on the seat of the Jeep, a shoulder propped against the door, his temple pressed against the frame of the window.

Puzzled, she strolled closer, then bent forward to squint into the dark car. With his hair tousled from the night's wind blowing through the opened window, he looked younger asleep. At least, she thought he was sleeping. One blue eye opened and stared at her.

"You were here all night?"

Slowly, he rubbed a hand over his bristly jaw, then rolled his shoulder against an ache. He viewed the stars that had popped up in the sky with the passing of the rain. A faint hint of dawn peeked at the horizon, but darkness shadowed the nearby trees. "Looks to me as if it's still night."

She couldn't help smiling. "Looks to me like you didn't sleep well."

Pushing up, he drew in the scent of both the early morning air and her. "Well enough."

"Are you playing my personal bodyguard?"

"Seemed like a good idea."

I'll take care of you, he'd told her once. *We'll take care of each other,* she'd assured him. "I'll be all right now. Go get a good night's sleep."

Didn't she know he'd never have slept at all anywhere else? Though he didn't want to alarm her, Seaton had been spotted only a mile away. That he'd traveled that close into town and had risked being caught made Jake damn nervous. Seaton had no reason to take such a chance unless he was trying to reach her. "I'll follow you into town first."

As he reached through the open window and toyed with a strand of her hair, she wanted to hold him. The need had nothing to do with desire, nothing to do with feeling safe. "Thank you."

Letting the strands slip through his fingers, he cracked a drowsy grin. "My pleasure."

* * *

A couple hours' sleep in a bed had helped. Showered and shaved, Jake drove from his motel to Henry's office. The lawyer looked less than pleased to see him again. His feigned, polite smile gave way to a scowl by the time Jake had finished with his question. Abby's power made Linser loyal to her, but he wouldn't turn away a client, not even a Ryker.

"You'd have a legal right to see that report," Henry assured Jake. "But, of course, it could take time."

Jake tapped an angry beat against his outer thigh. Abby's attorneys would block his every move, eating up years before he'd get the report released through the legal system.

"I do have some good news, though, As I mentioned before, the bank is interested in your property," he said with the enthusiasm of someone who'd already spent his check. "We need to make an appointment with Mark."

Jake never expected anything to be easy in Pineview. He wondered how much Wendley would let personal feelings interfere with business. "Set it up."

Needing to relax, he returned to the motel only long enough to change into jogging clothes. He pounded down the dirt road that led into the woods, and for the first time in his life, he considered breaking the law. Getting into the room behind the cells that stored old files wouldn't be difficult. Security systems in Pineview were nonexistent.

The idea was fleeting. He might get the report, but what would he prove, except that he was his old man's son? He couldn't blow it now—he'd worked too damn hard to live down the disgrace attached to the Ryker name and earn a reputation as an honest cop. He'd have to think of another way.

Habits die hard. Squinting against the setting sun, he left the dirt road and paced himself slower as he hit Main Street. Like he'd done hundreds of times, he ran with one destination in mind—McCall's Diner and Leigh.

Leigh calculated her last ticket and swept a glance around the room. Kathleen had left early for a dinner date, and Uncle Matt had disappeared fifteen minutes ago with his bowling-ball bag in hand. Reassured the waitresses on the evening shift had control of everything until her uncle returned, Leigh snatched up the paperback she'd tucked behind the counter earlier and headed for the door. The Widow Grentham had a date with a book.

Sunglasses in hand, she stepped outside. Leaning against the lamppost, his face glowing, his hair shining, Jake sent her a slow-forming smile. Her heart turned. How many times had she rushed from the diner and into his arms, knowing he'd be waiting for her just like this?

"I owe you a meal."

As his eyes locked with hers, temptation taunted her to touch the beads of perspiration on his forehead. "The diner's open." She managed to sound casual, but felt breathless.

"The diner?" He gave her a tolerant grin. "As much as I like the food there, isn't there a new Italian restaurant?"

Leigh fingered the strap on her purse. "It's swanky."

"Give me half an hour," he said, glancing down at his sweat-stained shirt.

"Give you..." Leigh said the words to his back. He was already running down the street.

Giorgio's catered to well-heeled tourists, but locals willing to shed Levi's for dressier clothes showed up for special occasions.

Ivy clung to the arched doorway outside the large white building. The soft, lilting music of a violin greeted patrons inside the entrance. Tiny lights sparkled from bare tree branches and more glittered overhead on the outside patio dining area.

"Pineview's gotten classy," Jake muttered at the sight of the waiter in a tuxedo.

Leigh accepted his guiding hand on her arm. "A new subdivision with a man-made lake and a golf course demanded more than McCall's Diner."

"Where's the golf course at?" he asked as they followed the maître d'.

Leigh turned puzzled eyes up at him. "You play golf?"

"Yeah, I do." Discreetly he drew her closer so their hips brushed. "Funny, isn't it. We have a lot of history, but—" he paused, his eyes capturing hers as they reached the table "—there's a lot we could learn."

It made no sense, but her heart jumped. Guilt, she thought. There was no other excuse for the reaction. She held a secret close to her heart, one she'd debated sharing with him ever since he'd arrived in town. For days, she'd agonized, running words through her head, then discarding them, aware there was no easy way to tell him about the months after he'd left. "I told you we've changed, Jake."

"Are you less understanding, less caring, less funny?" he asked, reaching across the table for her hand.

Just not so honest, anymore. A small frown creased a line between her brows. "I wasn't funny. I'm the serious sister."

"Made *me* laugh."

Leigh forced herself to relax, but for good measure, she slipped her hand free of his and picked up the menu. "When?"

"When you took forever to decide what you wanted to eat."

She peeked over the menu at him. "I don't do that."

"Know what you want?"

"Not yet."

Smiling, he lounged back in his chair, expecting her lengthy perusal of the menu. It was part of her nature to contemplate too long. He supposed that's what perplexed him the most about her marriage. It had happened so quickly. The Leigh he knew wouldn't have jumped into a vow of forever. Pressure? he wondered. With him out of the picture, had her father pressured her to marry his deputy? That time in her life was something they hadn't really hashed out.

Leigh settled on linguine alla scampi. As he ordered veal marsala, she recalled he used to eat ridiculous things for breakfast—tacos, vegetable soup, trout and coleslaw. "What happened to you during those ten years you were away?"

Only one answer came to mind, because it had been so instrumental in directing his life. "I found out I wasn't like my father. For years, I doubted myself. Everyone was always saying how much I was like him."

"You looked like him, but that's all."

He nudged aside the small vase and the carnations blocking his view of her. "People said you were blinded by love."

Hadn't she been more alert back then to the sounds of birds, to the brightness of the sun, to even the slightest flutter of the breeze, as if all her senses had sharpened? "I always thought love made a person see more clearly."

"A romantic thinks that way."

Leigh smoothed the mauve napkin in her lap. "I'm no romantic."

"Yes, you are. You were a sucker for romantic movies and mushy greeting cards." Faint lines crinkled at the corners of his eyes. "Do you still read the ending of a book first?"

"I always want to know how something will end before I begin." No one could foresee the future, but, innately, she wanted as many reassurances as she could get.

Across the candlelight, he saw vulnerability in her delicate features. Though patience rarely came easy to him, he understood the fragile thread he was tight-roping with her. In his occupation, no guarantees could be offered, but somehow he had to convince her that whatever they could have was better than noth-ing. "Do you know what I remembered most?"

Expecting some heart-wrenching memory, Leigh braced herself for more reminiscing that included some of the happiest and some of the most painful days of her life.

"Anchovies," he said when the waiter disappeared from their table.

"Anchovies?"

Jake pulled a disgusted face. "On pizza."

Leigh felt a tug on her heart. This was one of the reasons she'd fallen in love with him. He'd read her so well and had cajoled or demanded or comforted at precisely the right moment, as if he'd been inside her and had known what she'd craved most. "You don't know what you're missing."

"Yes, I do. Heartburn."

They shared a smile, a look, a fleeting moment when nothing mattered but being together. The invis-ible bond tightened. Leigh poked a fork into a shrimp. Effortlessly he could sweep all sensibility away from her, make her yearn for what could be. But too much had happened to each of them, too much time had passed. "Tell me what you did after you left town."

He'd wandered like a man with no country, no soul.
Even today, he didn't have a home. He occupied an
apartment, he owned no pets and barely any furni-
ture beyond a bed and a television. He put in long days
at work, then spent half his free time working out,
going to the shooting range and taking classes in
criminal law. He had no ambition to be a lawyer, but
he had craved the knowledge. "The highlight of my
life back then was a job washing dishes. It lasted two
days."

Curling her fingers around the stem of the wine-
glass, she listened to his humorous anecdote. "You
broke all of the dishes?" she asked with a laugh.

"Close. The woman who owned the restaurant politely told me I wasn't meant to be a dishwasher. Too
clumsy."

Leigh looked down at her plate to veil her thoughts.
Never had there been anything clumsy about his caresses. "And then?"

Jake forked another of the veal medallions, but
eating was the last thing on his mind. His body felt
tense, his stomach tight, as he wondered if she'd fit as
perfectly against him as she had before. "Then I got
a job on a grill at a fast-food restaurant. I worked
there while going to school."

She tilted her head, and candlelight danced across
her face. She looked beautiful. The dress she'd chosen was a royal blue, a shiny material that dipped low
enough in front to bother him. It bothered him a lot
as he caught the hint of lace beneath it. "I missed a lot
years ago." His voice softened more with intimacy.

"You're even more lovely in candlelight. I should have taken you someplace romantic years ago."

Hadn't she thought back then that every place they'd been together had been special and romantic? "How easily you forget," she said lightly to keep the mood that way. He doubted he'd forgotten even one second he'd spent with her.

"That pizza parlor we went to had candles on the tables."

Softly he chuckled. "It was a dive."

"It wasn't a dive," she countered, not willing to let him snatch away a wonderful remembrance for her.

"Stubs of candles were stuck in wine bottles, Leigh."

"I remember it as very romantic."

"What else do you remember?"

Wanting you with me forever, she reflected as she stared at the fork in her hand. "Fun times," she admitted honestly, recalling all the laughter shared.

A smile softened his features. "Yeah, we had a lot of them."

In silence, they finished their meal. He could talk to her about anything and everything. What he couldn't bear to share were the years of bone-aching loneliness he'd felt, when it seemed a slice of himself had stayed behind with her.

Mellow, Leigh excused herself and slipped into the rest room. Staring in the mirror, she faced the emotion she'd been dodging since his return. Love. She'd never stopped loving him.

A hand in his pocket, Jake sidestepped customers strolling in from outside and strolled to the window in the restaurant's anteroom. A sliver of moon peeked from behind slow-moving clouds. Not in years had he contemplated the future. He'd lived moment to moment, but suddenly everything he wanted was within his grasp.

"Jake." Dressed in a flowery summer dress, Kathleen gave the impression of a woman a decade younger than thirty.

"You really don't look like a mother of two," he said, smiling. But he had already noted the seriousness in her brown eyes.

"I've wanted to talk to you. I..." She hesitated as if unsure how to proceed. "Jake, don't hurt her again," she said in what sounded more like a plea than a warning.

"Kathleen, what happened before is history."

Her head reared back slightly, as if he'd poked at her. "She didn't write it all off so easily. I watched the pain my sister went through when you left without even a goodbye. Do you know how humiliated she was? She'd believed in you, in your promises, and you left without a care that you'd broken all of them," she said passionately. "People knew she cared about you. They knew you dumped her."

"Dumped her! Is that what all of you think?" He pulled back his own temper to keep his voice quiet, their conversation private. "I didn't dump her."

"No, you simply left her."

Jake drew a hard, steadying breath to battle the years of bitterness exploding inside him. "I was escorted out of town, dammit, by your father."

Steps from them, Leigh froze.

A mixture of regret and incredulity settled on Kathleen's face. "Leigh never told me that."

"I didn't tell her." He damned himself instantly for saying anything now, but he'd felt defensive. "She didn't need to know," he said quickly, hoping Kathleen wouldn't persist.

"But she does. Why don't you tell her?"

Leigh stepped closer. "What are you talking about?"

As her questioning eyes met his, walls closed in on him. "Never mind."

"I want to know."

Kathleen touched her arm in a soothing gesture. "Leigh, people are looking."

She shook off Kathleen's grip. "I don't care." She fixed a look on him, trying to see beyond his cool, almost-expressionless gaze. "Answer me."

"Let's get out of here first," he said with a firmness that allowed for no opposition.

Mechanically Leigh moved, waiting only until they'd stepped outside. "You said my father made you leave."

This was something he'd never planned to do. He parroted his previous words. "That's right. He told me to get out of town."

Disbelief edged her voice. "Are you telling me that my father bullied you?"

"Call it what you want." He measured how much to say. There was still a chance he wouldn't have to reveal everything and destroy a loving memory for her. "I was nineteen years old, and he was the law."

"He told you to leave, so you did?"

"Yeah. I did what I was told," he said, simplifying that night ten years ago.

"No." Attuned to him, Leigh perceived it wasn't so simple. "There's more. You never did anything unless you wanted to or you absolutely had to." She paused, needing an answer, yet almost afraid to hear his. "What happened?"

"Leigh, forget it." She was in a temper. He'd faced it before, sometimes meeting it head-on, sometimes cajoling her out of the mood. "I didn't want to go, but I did."

Frustration welled up inside her. "Tell me. Please," she appealed, reaching out and touching his cheek.

One touch. It slammed every emotion back at him that he'd smothered on that night ten years ago—the fear, the outrage, the unhappiness. "Why don't you just forget you heard anything?"

Leigh searched his eyes, and she knew. He was trying to protect her. "Do you know how important you were to me? Do you know how much I cried? I never understood why you'd left." She drew her fingers along his cheek. "Jake, I need the truth."

With a silent oath, he looked away.

"Do you want me to beg?"

"Stop it." He swung back and found himself pinned by the dark eyes he'd longed to see every day of his life. "He told me if I didn't leave he'd arrest me."

"Arrest you?"

As her fingers clung relentlessly to his arm, he knew there was no way to dodge the truth. "He'd file statutory rape charges against me."

She felt her stomach lurch and swallowed hard as bile rose in her throat.

"I was a kid, Leigh." His hands on her upper arms, he pulled her closer. More than anything, he wanted her to understand. "I was scared. I left. I thought once I got a job and a place to stay, you would come and be with me. But when I called my father, you were married already. End of plan."

She was breathing hard, still trying to absorb what he'd just told her. He wouldn't lie, not about that.

"Why do you think I didn't meet you at the lake? I loved you. I'd have died for you. But we wouldn't have had much of a future if I was sitting in jail."

"Oh, my God." Sagging back against the wall, she closed her eyes, lost years flashing through her mind. Her father *had* kept Jake's letter from her. He'd chased him away. He'd taken everything she'd wanted from her. Why? Why had he been so against Jake? He'd never been in any real trouble. There had been no reason for her father's actions, except that Jake was a Ryker.

Her throat tight, she fought anger. She needed to think, to understand. Her father would have done nothing without her aunt's knowledge. "Drive me to the diner."

For the moment, he backed away from drawing her close. She wanted answers, not sympathy. But beneath the pale light of the moon, she looked white, her eyes darkened by hurt as much as anger. "Leigh, forget it."

She couldn't. Though there was no point questioning her aunt, her uncle wouldn't brush her off.

Quietly, steadily, Leigh maneuvered her uncle into the office at the back of the diner.

A smile played on his lips at being whisked out of the restaurant. "What in the world could be so important that we needed to—"

Leigh interrupted. "Do you know why Jake left town?"

Amusement died in his eyes. "Did he tell you?"

Leigh was in no mood for a game of words. The dear man standing near had a gentle spirit, a kind one. He'd been the baby in a family of a domineering sister and a strong-willed brother. She knew he wasn't the culprit, but he must have known. "You did know what my father did, didn't you?"

Lines deepened in his face as he sighed heavily. "Leigh, that happened years ago. Why bring up something that...?" Pausing, he held out an appealing hand to her. "I know he loved you dearly."

"It's true that he threatened Jake?" she asked, barely able to get the words out. A glance away and silence spoke volumes. "Uncle Matt, why didn't you tell me?"

"I couldn't. I love you like a daughter. I knew how important Jake was to you. If you'd followed him, if you'd left, your father would have filed the charges against him."

Oh, how innocent, how young, how blind she'd been then. "So he and Aunt Abby even controlled you?"

A vise gripped the base of Leigh's neck. Strolling out of the diner, she pressed fingers to it and kneaded, trying to loosen tense muscles. She needed quiet, someplace to consider all she'd learned. But the leaves whispering beneath the warm night breeze, the chirping of crickets, the faint sound of music drifting out from someone's stereo intruded, making her struggle to think. Her father, the man she'd trusted the most, had snatched away her dreams. Out of love? How could a person hurt another in the name of love? How could he have deliberately broken her heart, stolen a piece of her soul?

Waiting for her, Jake stepped closer. He didn't need to see her face. Her slender back was rigid.

"I thought so badly of you." She wanted to scream as tears smarted the backs of her eyes. "How could he do that?"

"I don't know," he said, because he had no words of comfort. Gathering her close, he simply held her.

* * *

Weary, Leigh laid her head back on the seat of the Jeep. She listened to the hum of the engine, concentrated on each bump in the road. In the distance, she heard the wailing signal of an approaching train. Thoughts kept whirling around in her mind. Since Jake's return, she'd kept a shield in place, believing only a foolish woman allowed the same man to hurt her twice. Only he'd been hurt, too.

He'd been a boy, railroaded out of town by the sheriff—by her father. There had been no one for him to turn to. He'd once told her that there had never been anyone in his life he could depend on but her. Even she had failed him. She hadn't waited, couldn't wait. And he'd loved her as much as he'd said he had. He hadn't left her. He'd never wanted to leave her.

A passing car's headlight glared in her eyes, blinding her view of her house before Jake turned into her driveway. Numb. She felt so numb. "I wish I could understand," she said during their stroll to the porch. "If I— If we knew why, if there was a reason . . ." She stopped her rambling. There was no excuse for what her father had done.

The wind tossed her hair forward, a curtain framing her face while moonlight emphasized her paleness. "You'll never know," he said, damning his own inadequacies.

But she had to learn why her father had betrayed the trust she'd had in him, why he'd abandoned values he'd taught her and Kathleen.

"It's over, Leigh."

Nothing was. Staring at him, she sensed that what she'd once felt—still felt—might never be over. "I could use a hug." The words weren't necessary. His arms were already around her. Sliding her hands up his back, she relaxed against him. "Will you stay?"

It would have been easy to misinterpret her request. Pulling back, he saw in the dim light what he wanted to see. Desire in her dark eyes. An invitation in her parted lips. He wanted to latch on to her words, but he knew better. Emotions running high, she was too vulnerable. And once he touched her again and felt her willingness, he wouldn't walk away. "I'll be outside in the Jeep," he assured her. "If you need me—"

"No, I meant stay," she whispered, linking her fingers with his before he could move away. They stepped into the house. "I want to banish every bad moment from my mind." Lightly she kissed his knuckles. "I want this night with you, the one we should have had ten years ago." Staring up at him, she started to unbutton his shirt. "I want you tonight."

He didn't move, almost afraid he was fantasizing and the slightest move would snatch away everything.

At his silence, she slid a hand around his neck. "Do you want me?"

"Want you? I ache for you," he whispered.

As his hands framed her face, she felt a breath catch in her throat. She wanted the pain gone. She wanted the joy, the gentleness she'd had only with him. She didn't speak. Her heart pounding, she urged and answered the mouth slanting across hers. Tongues tasted and blended with whispery words, and the anger inside her, the disappointment, the heartache, eased. He could always make her forget. He could always comfort her. "Don't leave me," she murmured, realizing those were words she'd have said to him years ago if she'd had the chance.

"Never again." His arms around her, he kicked the door open, and together they stepped into the house. He'd been dead inside before this, he realized as he took his fill of the sweetness he'd once been addicted to.

In the dark room, a hunger swept over him as a fantasy he'd harbored for too many years was finally blending with reality. He tempered his needs to stretch out the moment, to absorb every second. Silk moved under his touch and gave way to his hand. He caressed her bare shoulders, flesh that was as soft as he remembered, softer than anything he'd ever felt.

Her mouth clinging to his, she heard the whisper of cloth falling from her. Sensations slithered along her skin as his hand skimmed downward from her breast to her thigh.

Each kiss, each brush of his fingers, bound them again. Her head light, she wondered when they'd moved as he pressed an arm to her back and sank them down to the sofa. For too long, she'd lived on memories. But there was no yesterday now, and she was still sane enough to acknowledge that there would be no tomorrows. Whatever happened between them, there would be no dreams, no plans, no promises. She wouldn't allow herself to have them.

This was enough, she decided, seeking the zipper on his pants, pushing the slacks from his hips, shoving them with her feet down his legs. Flesh met flesh. It was magic as the hard length of his body pressed against hers.

She reached for him. She wasn't the shy young girl he'd known. She was a woman with needs and wants, and a desire to please as much as receive pleasure. She stroked and caressed, matching his every move, offering all she could to him—to the one man, the only man, she'd ever love.

Kiss for kiss, touch for touch. Neither of them led nor followed. Pleasure echoed in each kiss, each caress. Shuddering beneath the warmth of his hand, she thought she'd go mad as the heat of his mouth and the moistness of his tongue enticed her breasts, her belly, her inner thighs.

All the youthful dreams buried for years sprang alive within her. Arching against his hand, she felt the rightness of the moment, welcomed the excitement she'd known with him before. Passion weaved around them, skin turned slick with it, yet it was love inciting every kiss, every move.

And tenderly he urged her to journey with him. Eyes tight, she grew wild beneath his hands until her body, not her mind, ruled. Lightning quick, a rush swept over her, and desperation coiled inside her. She needed him. She needed the oneness that bound hearts as well as bodies.

Madness slipping over him, he rode an edge of control, even as urgency surged through him. Savor.

He caressed soft hot inner flesh, tasted her, felt her skin quiver. In his mind, nothing seemed like enough. Lost in her, a senselessness took over. Raw desire dueled with a lover's patience. The promise of more pleasure mingled with an undeniable ache as he lowered himself to her. For a heart-stopping moment, while poised over her, he stared down at the face that had haunted his dreams, that had made every other woman pale in comparison, and then he slipped into her.

And with her heat enveloping him, he gave in, letting the frenzy take control. His mouth on hers, he took her with him this time. He knew this was how it should have always been. Moving as one, they clung to each other. No one could separate them this time. No one, he vowed, before the world exploded.

Chapter Nine

He awoke needing her. Seconds passed before it registered that he hadn't dreamed everything, that her
head was resting on his chest. At one moment last
night, he'd thought he would stop breathing and die
with a smile on his face. The feel of her heart pounding in rhythm with his was a sound that had seemed
lost to him forever. Now, with her snuggling close, her
slender leg tangling with his, he burned again for her.
"I dreamed about you like this," he said softly as,
feather light, his lips grazed her jaw.

Leigh sighed as much from the gentleness of his
mouth as from her thoughts. It was becoming more
difficult to think of a good reason why they couldn't
be together. He'd always been everything she'd
wanted—strong, intelligent, thoughtful and roman-

tic. "I didn't want this, Jake." The protest came out weak.

"But you do." He lifted her hair to kiss the curve of her neck.

God help her, she did.

"I never forgot you."

Her eyes closed, she skimmed a finger along his side, down the lean, muscular flesh that she'd touched and tasted the night before. "For a while," she countered lightly, then supported herself on his chest to stare into his eyes. In the shadowy darkness of the room, they were so intense, so loving. Words clung to the tip of her tongue. She'd never say them. One night was all she'd planned. One time to remember, to end her mind's fantasy that no one else was as wonderful. But one time wasn't enough. She leaned forward, her lips playing across his chest. Inching down, she traced the line of hair down his belly.

With a stroke of her fingers, he caught his breath. "Never." The word was torn from his throat as strands of her hair brushed his thigh.

Waking slowly, Jake let a pleasurable dream slip away. He should have felt satisfied, more at peace, yet he wanted more. And he knew passion had nothing to do with the longing inside him.

With effort, he roused himself from the bed and tugged up his pants. Drawn to the rich smell of coffee and the music drifting through the rooms, he padded barefoot to the kitchen.

Leaning unobserved against the kitchen doorway, he absorbed the sight of her. She looked seventeen again. Her hair mussed from sleep and his hands, she stood before him in a knee-length shirt with a faded Daffy Duck on it. She was everything he'd remembered, and more than he'd ever imagined wanting again.

Her back to him, Leigh sensed him standing near. She poured coffee, amazed at having morning-after jitters, but she was experiencing a first. The first time she'd actually slept with him. The first time she'd awakened with him. The first time she'd faced the light of a new day with him.

Scanning the sparse offerings on the shelves of her refrigerator, she considered his eccentric breakfast choices and suggested the most disgusting thing to eat at five in the morning. "Want pickles and salmon?"

Jake pushed away from the doorway and dropped to a chair. He felt her nerves as she flitted around the room. Being with her had felt as comfortable as slipping into a second skin. "Had it yesterday."

Glancing over her shoulder, she caught his grin.

"Come here." He reached out and tugged her to his lap. Though he wanted to draw her against him, he waited, trying to read her as he had before. Too much time away made it harder. "Who's making you nervous? Seaton or me?"

She should have known she'd never fool him. "It shows?"

Jake skimmed her thigh with his fingers. "Just a little."

"This is different," she tried to explain. Feeling foolish, she laughed self-consciously. "We never slept together or woke up together."

"Yeah." His lips curved in a slow smile. "This is better."

Leigh rubbed her cheek against his. "This *is* better," she admitted softly.

"You know, they say that the more you do something, the more comfortable you feel about it." Eyes dancing with humor met hers as he pushed to a stand with her in his arms. "So we'll go back to bed and get up again later."

She giggled. She hadn't giggled since—since he'd disappeared from her life. "You aren't hungry?"

"Hungry?" A laugh wove into his voice. "I've been fasting for ten years," he said, crossing the bedroom in three strides and tumbling onto the bed with her.

"This is..." She sighed as his fingers gently played across her hip. Speaking seemed useless. She closed her eyes, already lost in the caress of his hand beneath her nightshirt.

"How the hell do you get up this early all the time?" At the stove, Jake yawned twice while he stirred eggs.

Leigh opened the back door to let the morning air into the kitchen. She was accustomed to waking in darkness and driving to town before most people had hit their alarm-clock Snooze button for the first time. With the diner opening at six, she and Kathleen always got there by five-thirty. "I'm used to it." She grimaced at the concoction in the frying pan. She recognized only scrambled eggs. "What time do you get up in the city?"

"Three in the afternoon."

"Three?"

"I work the night shift." He pushed the eggs around in the pan. "It's that kind of work."

"You and Dracula."

Softly he chuckled. "I never liked getting up early."

Because he'd always had to, she surmised. He'd worked at the supermarket for years, going there at four in the morning before school to stock shelves. "You should have stayed in bed."

"Couldn't do that."

Leigh cautiously sipped the steaming coffee in her cup. "Why not?"

"I'm on vacation."

She assumed he had good reasoning behind that statement but wasn't sure what it was. "Don't people usually sleep in when they're on vacation?"

"Because they have to get up early every day."

Pressing a hip against the stove, Leigh bit back a laugh. "So because you don't, you do on vacation?"

One hand holding the spatula, he caught her waist and nudged her closer. "Another reason."

"What is it?"

How could he make her realize that he'd cared about nothing without her? "To be with you." Lightly, gently he kissed her before pivoting away to snatch the pan from the burner.

Everything had been simple before, but now she knew she'd have to face him with the most difficult words she'd ever uttered in her life. They couldn't have secrets, not anymore. "Jake . . ."

She sounded too serious. For a little while, he wanted to enjoy the moments with her and exclude all problems, all of the sad memories, anything that might spoil their time together. "Got any hot sauce?"

Leigh shook her head. She couldn't get the words out. The moments with him were too precious to lose, and once she revealed everything about those months after he'd left, about her marriage, then all the loving moments might vanish forever.

"Do you get any days off from that job of yours?" he asked while rummaging through the refrigerator.

"I could get off a little early today."

Banging his hip against the refrigerator door to close it, he held the catsup bottle. "Name it. And we'll do whatever you want."

"A movie." Thoughtfully she stared at the floor, vowing to herself to tell him everything later.

"Earth to Leigh."

She raised a smile to him. "And an ice-cream cone after."

"You got it." A plate in his hand, he paused beside her and kissed the bridge of her nose. "Whatever you want," he said with more seriousness than she'd have imagined.

* * *

"As long as they don't lose the sock they'll find him," Jake told her while trailing her into the diner later.

"A sock?"

"Al has one of Seaton's socks wrapped in plastic in his office refrigerator. It preserves the scent." In passing, he skimmed a hand over the curve of her hip, then strode toward the office and back storeroom.

"You know this is silly, don't you?" she asked, looking up from starting the coffee brewer.

Like before, he paid no attention. Until Seaton was caught, he wasn't leaving her alone.

While she flicked on the rest of the lights, she listened to him opening and closing the doors. With a deep breath, she struggled to stifle her own uneasiness, but he'd set off an alarm inside her when he'd announced that he was waiting at the diner with her until her uncle arrived. Who knew better than a policeman when to be cautious? If Jake was worried, it was hard for her not to be. "I told you I won't be alone long. Kathleen will be here in a few minutes." In response to the sound of the bell above the door, Leigh swung around. "See," she said, motioning toward Kathleen, who was coming through the doorway a step ahead of their uncle.

Kathleen pulled up short. And as if he were at a tennis match, her uncle's head swiveled toward Leigh, then Jake, and back to her.

Leigh anticipated an interrogation the moment that Jake left.

Bracing his hands on the counter, he leaned across it and kissed her quickly. "Now I'll leave."

Absolute silence lingered even after the door clicked behind him. A frown wrinkled her uncle's brow, but he said nothing. As usual, Kathleen proved more vocal. "Okay, what's going on?"

"He's guarding me." Did she sound as casual as she hoped? Leigh wondered.

"Is that why you're glowing?"

Leigh dismissed her words with a backward sweep of her hand.

Hands on her hips, Kathleen positioned herself in front of Leigh. "Are you going to tell me what's going on?"

Truth seemed the easiest course.

In a slow, disbelieving motion, Kathleen shook her head as Leigh quickly reiterated what she'd learned last night about Jake's swift departure from town ten years ago. "I don't want to believe it."

"It's true. Uncle Matt admitted it. That's why Jake left."

Together, they settled on stools at the counter.

"I knew Dad didn't like you with him, but to do that—"

"I know." Leigh gripped her sister's hand. Suddenly everything they'd always believed in seemed false. To them, their father had been a paragon of truth and justice. She'd had more time than Kathleen to accept the facts, but was still wrestling with the same emotion she'd felt ever since she'd learned the truth. "I can't believe it, either."

"Oh, Leigh, everything you went through—you didn't have to," Kathleen said sadly.

Leigh didn't want to think too much about her marriage to Ken, about afterward. "I tried to tell him everything, Kathleen. I don't know how."

"So now what?"

Leigh shrugged, not having any answers.

Inside the redbrick building that housed the town's jail, the honorable mayor was kicking back in a chair opposite Al.

As if they were old friends, Tebner rose to welcome Jake. "You're just the man I wanted to see."

Warily, Jake strolled closer. "About what?"

"Al, here," Tebner started with a sweep of his arm in the deputy's direction, "told me you've been suggesting some ideas for catching Seaton. You know, Jake," he said softly, conspiratorially, though only the three of them were in the room. "We'd really like Pineview to get credit for catching Seaton."

"Makes sense." He shot a quick, amused look at Al. The man's round face broadened with a humorous grin. Jake supposed he looked baffled at Tebner's congeniality, but no one would have given him the time of day ten years ago. And here he was, receiving a friendly pat on the back while Tebner relayed what he considered confidential information.

"Like you advised, we'll have Eddie watch Seaton's sister."

Like he advised? Somehow he managed a poker face while Tebner rambled on. Jake wanted to laugh.

Since returning to town, some fairy godmother must have passed her magic wand over him. What else could explain his transformation in everyone's eyes from town hoodlum to the fair-haired boy?

Leigh set a plate before one of the men from a construction crew. He was scooping his fork into the roast beef and mashed potatoes before she turned away. Waiting for an order, Kathleen was debating with the cook about the teams that were destined for the World Series. Leigh glanced at the clock. She had thirty minutes before Jake came to pick her up. It was enough time. "I'm going out," she said at an opportune moment.

Puzzlement knitted a frown line between Kathleen's brows.

"I won't be long," Leigh assured her.

Her sister's eyes sliced to the small bouquet of flowers that Leigh had retrieved from an unused cold case under the counter. "What about Jake?"

"I'll be back before he knows I've left."

"But—"

Leigh raised a halting hand. "I need to go, Kathleen."

With ten minutes left before Leigh's shift ended, Jake strolled into the diner, anticipating drinking several cups of coffee while he waited. Settling on a stool, he noticed only a handful of customers.

Plates in her hands, Kathleen rounded the counter and smiled. She looked tired but not harried.

"Where's your sister?"

"She said you two were going to a movie later."

He'd been a cop too long not to spot evasiveness instantly. "She's probably chosen some B horror flick," he said, going along with her for the moment. Jake waited until she'd delivered the orders and was strolling back. "So where is she now?"

Almost lazily, Kathleen moved her shoulders. "She might have gone home. We're not really busy."

"Gone home?" His mind clicked off possibilities. The most frightening one revolved around her running into Seaton. None of it made sense. Why would she go home? She was supposed to wait for him. He fastened a hard look on Kathleen. "Where is she?"

Nervously, she glanced away. He'd seen them cover for each other before, but they weren't great liars.

"Where, Kathleen?"

Indecision flickered across her face. "The cemetery," she said softly.

Jake floored the gas pedal as soon as he reached the town's limits. Fuming, he lit a cigarette, tossed it out the Jeep window, then lit another. She was supposed to stay put until he got back. She didn't have to leave, dammit. He'd have driven her to the cemetery. Did she think he was so enraged by her father's antics, such an insensitive bastard, that he'd refuse her if she wanted to visit his grave or Ken Grentham's?

Easing the car onto the drive bordered by rose bushes, he saw her kneeling, her head bent as she set down a bouquet of carnations.

Certain she was safe, he parked and finished his cigarette to give her privacy. As the landscaped grounds darkened with dusk, a light evening breeze fluttered a chill across the arm he'd propped on the window ledge. By waiting, he'd reined in his temper. Still, he took his time. In a slow stride, he passed the rows of bouquets placed on the markers of loved ones and wound a path to her.

The wind ruffled her hair, but Leigh didn't move. From the corner of her eye, she saw Jake coming closer. This wasn't the way she'd wanted to tell him. Her throat tight, she feared she'd strangle from guilt. She'd waited too long. She should have told him, should have found the right words.

Unsure of her mood, he remained quiet and squatted beside her to read the inscription etched on the grave marker. *Alan—beloved son—Heart's desire, here and gone one November morn.* A moment passed, no longer than a second, but it slipped away in such slow motion it felt like an hour as the date engraved on her child's marker flashed back at him. *November*.

Shaken, he sat back on his heels and stretched for a breath as realization slithered over him. She'd been eight months pregnant when she'd lost the baby. He'd still been in town in May. "Alan." He spoke so softly, the word came out on a whisper.

Hearing him speak that name nearly crumbled her. With a shake of her head, she fought the smarting behind her eyes. Unlike others, he'd know the significance of the name. She'd chosen his middle name, because she hadn't been able to use his last.

Excruciatingly slow, his gaze came back to her. "Mine?"

Leigh waited a moment, but afraid to do more, she barely moved her head in a nod. What was he thinking? Did he blame her?

Heavy, unbearable pressure built up inside his chest. "You said you couldn't wait."

"I thought you weren't coming back." Why did what seemed so logical then sound empty of feeling now? "I never got the letter. I hadn't heard from you." She hugged herself as the breeze shivered her suddenly. "I missed you so," she whispered.

A pain pierced him, and it seemed so real, he winced.

"The night you left I'd planned to tell you I was pregnant." She grappled for words. "When Ken told my father he wanted to marry me, he and my aunt pressured me—for the family's sake. A quick wedding, they said. There would be whispers, but no one would know for sure. I didn't think you'd come back," she said, not for the first time, remembering her anguish at never seeing him again. "So I agreed."

Clamminess bathed the back of his neck. He stared at the ground, then at the words again. A child. He'd had a child.

"I tried to be a good wife, but Ken knew I never really loved him. I was—" She couldn't say more. She couldn't look at him any longer, couldn't stand the pain mirrored in his eyes that she'd harbored within herself for so long.

"Like me," he said, feeling a sadness he'd never known before. "You were scared."

Leigh took a painfully hard breath. "Yes. And after—after I lost the baby, I was devastated."

Jake fought the pressure crowding his throat and chest. He'd never felt that he'd had any real family. Life had tossed him another curve. Ten years ago, he could have had one, a wife and a child.

Lightly he ran his fingertips across the words on the marker. No, they wouldn't have had this child. But he still damned everyone who'd interfered. Because of them, she'd endured this loss alone. They'd taken more than he'd expected. They'd taken his right to be here for her. Though she'd lost their baby, he'd had rights—the right to comfort, to mourn.

Leigh remained silent. There was nothing to say to exonerate herself for keeping this secret, to ease this loss for him. In a few seconds, she'd given and she'd taken away from him. "I'm sorry. I'm sorry I lost your baby. I'm sorry I didn't tell you, but..." She gathered courage to quiet the tremble in her voice. "I dealt with everything the only way I knew how. And when you showed up, what could I say? The baby I lost was yours? I couldn't blurt those words out."

As if she were fragile as glass, Jake touched her shoulders lightly. "I'm not blaming you, dammit. I blame myself for not being here." Slipping an arm around her shoulder, he drew her to a stand. For a long moment, he concentrated on the sounds around

him—the birds chirping, the rustle of leaves beneath
the breeze. "What..." He paused and looked at the
marker. "What happened?"

Leigh stared down at the summery green ground.
The warmth of the sun pressed down on her, but she
shivered as if the bite of winter's chill rippled across
her flesh. "It was winter, icy. I fell." All the pain from
that terrible November morning stirred fresh inside
her. Mourning again, she pressed fingers to the corners of her eyes. "I went into premature labor. He was
alive for only a moment," she murmured. "I—I heard
him cry."

Leigh tried to turn from Jake, to get away. After all
this time, she was feeling the emptiness again, as if a
slice of her heart had been cut away. She didn't want
to feel it again, hadn't expected it to hurt so badly.
And she longed to escape his stare because it made the
memories so alive she could smell the small white tea
roses that she'd placed on the tiny casket.

There were no words. All he could do was hold her
as he should have ten years ago.

Tears fell as all the buried sorrow for her child re-
surfaced. Leigh clung to him. She felt his soothing
touch on her hair, and knew this was what she hadn't
had when she'd lost his child. No sympathy from others had reached her. She'd needed his arms and his
strength. She'd needed to hang on to the only person
who could really share her pain—her baby's father.

Unlike some silences, the one between them during
the drive to her house bonded them. She considered all

she'd lost. She'd been scared to tell him the truth, frightened not of losing him but of him hating her, not understanding what she'd done and why. Most of all, she'd worried he wouldn't know what she'd felt. But in that one instant when he'd pulled her into his arms, he'd given her something she hadn't expected. Peace. For years, she'd mourned their child alone. As long as he hadn't known about the baby, she hadn't felt totally at peace over the loss.

Jake braked in front of her house. For her, he'd weather his own grief during moments alone. "I don't know what else to say to you except I'm sorry. You shouldn't have had to go through that alone."

It was more than she'd hoped for. Shifting on the seat, she touched his cheek. "You've already said what I needed to hear."

"No, I haven't. I love you." A lingering sadness dulled his eyes. "Do you believe me?"

"Jake. We—"

"Belong together," he said roughly, still fighting anger at all that had been taken from them. "I love you. I've never stopped." His hands trapping her face, he held it still and searched her eyes. "Never, never stopped."

Chapter Ten

They forgot about the movie, a night meant for lighthearted fun. In his arms, she spoke of those days she'd passed in a sleepless haze, enduring a waking nightmare. Truth. It cleansed the soul. It made what they'd once had a part of them again. He'd always been the one she'd told everything to, the one who'd listened and accepted everything about her. He'd never placed any conditions on their love. Facing a new day with him, she knew he still wouldn't, but she couldn't say the same.

Morning sunlight glared against the window of the Jeep. Jake drove through town, past the diner, and considered the strength of the woman sitting beside him. He ached for her, for himself. What had been lost couldn't be found. But they could start over.

Turning down a street, he wheeled the car into the parking lot adjacent to the hospital. No amount of persuasion had convinced Leigh to forego volunteering at the hospital as she did every week.

Hours later, Jake slouched on a chair, thumbed through another magazine and waited. Wherever she went, he planned to be near. For as long as Seaton eluded capture, he represented a danger to her.

Resting his head against the wall, Jake inhaled the antiseptic smell and recalled the night they'd wheeled him in on a gurney. Heat searing his right shoulder, he'd drifted in and out of consciousness. In a hazy stupor, he'd heard the doctors and nurses, his partner cussing someone, and he'd mentally smiled.

When he'd awakened, he'd learned his father had died. He'd spent the first week out of the hospital in a foul mood, stymied by a damaged wing whenever he'd tried to dress or cook. It wasn't the first time he'd been shot. Work in narcotics meant facing off with the worst of mankind, those who were high on drugs or desperate for them or greedy for the money they'd bring.

He knew the risks in his work, but rarely thought about them. If a cop got scared, he lost the edge. He'd never considered the danger until he'd seen the fear reflected in Leigh's eyes when she'd told him about the day her father and Grentham had been shot. But there was no changing who he was now, any more than he could change her. The future looked grim—too grim.

* * *

Daylight hours passed uneventfully. As night descended, lights flicked on around him. Outside the wall of windows, the wind howled, as if emphasizing the incoming storm. Sipping lukewarm coffee, he zeroed in on Leigh breezing out of double doors.

"We got a call," she yelled, whizzing past him. "A car accident."

Jake tossed the cup and its contents into the closest receptacle and trailed her down a corridor, matching her clipped pace.

"Don't get in the way," she warned.

He ignored her brief, stinging look. "Don't get cranky."

Leigh gentled her mood before she scooted into the ambulance. She had no reason for being angry. He was only trying to protect her, but that emphasized what she'd been intent on forgetting. Men who protected risked their lives.

The accident wasn't bad. Only shaken and bruised, the driver, who'd made an illegal turn in a pickup truck and broadsided a station wagon, stood on the shoulder of the highway, answering Eddie's questions. An ambulance transferred the family of tourists to the hospital.

Jake arrived at the emergency entrance behind Eddie's cruiser and watched Leigh hustle behind a gurney toward the emergency tunnel.

"I hate highway accidents," Eddie grumbled, catching up with Jake on the steps. "Everyone's upset. It takes hours to make sense of what happened. Then there's reports up the backside to file.''

Understandingly Jake nodded. Paperwork dogged him in the city, too.

''Al told me that Hamil and his men think Seaton's gone.''

They were all wrong. Jake felt it in his gut.

He hit the emergency room doors and the waiting room, then strode toward the double doors and pushed them open to look in. Amid the sea of doctors and nurses scurrying around, he didn't see Leigh. He charged in. Behind him, a nurse called out some prattle about hospital rules. He didn't give a damn.

He whisked through the room and out, having to skirt the sour-looking nurse. At full speed, he slammed through the doors toward the long tunnel that led from the emergency parking lot to the hospital and nearly plowed into an ambulance attendant sipping a soda by the vending machine.

Then he saw her. Standing by it, she was handing a candy bar to a little boy while she murmured soft, reassuring words to him. Jake stopped, but he couldn't halt an image of her with another child—his child.

He'd be incredibly handsome one day, Leigh thought, kneeling beside the boy. He wasn't the first child she'd seen brought into emergency, but he was the right age and the right coloring to be her child. She was sure he'd have grown up with dark hair, thick and touched with red like his father's. She wondered often if he'd have had the same disturbing blue eyes, the high cheekbones, the smile that softened his features with friendliness. She'd always wonder, she realized. She'd always imagine what he'd have looked like grown up.

Swallowing the knot of emotion in her throat, Leigh responded to footsteps behind her and sent the boy's mother a friendly smile. "He's fine," she assured her before turning away to leave them alone.

Lounging against a wall, Jake took a second to sweep a quick look over, needing reassurance that she wasn't harmed. "I was looking all over the place in there for you."

As he slashed the air in the direction of the emergency room, she noted that more than annoyance colored his voice. "I worried you?"

With something that sounded more like a snort than a laugh, he sent her a look of incredulity. "You could say that." He wanted to hold her. He knew she was safe, but he wanted to feel her in his arms. Then there would be no doubts. And he knew now what she felt, what she feared. The panic, the uncertainty, the helplessness. And how easy it was to overreact.

Leigh understood more than he could imagine. She'd experienced her share of such moments for others. "Could I buy you a cup of coffee?" she asked to measure his mood.

Drawing her into the crook of his shoulder, for both their sakes, he made a stab at humor. "I think I know what the doctor would order for you."

Relaxing, she affectionately jabbed his rib with her elbow. "I bet you do."

*   *   *

The grandfather clock signaled midnight as hamburgers sizzled in a frying pan. Beside him, Leigh flipped the meat patties. "They're almost done."

At the kitchen counter, Jake sliced tomatoes with more force than necessary. A helplessness he'd never known before had enveloped him during those brief moments when he'd searched for her. Oddly, he understood her fear now. Because she'd been out of his sight, he'd been frantic that something might have happened to her.

Fighting off a dark uneasiness, he rolled his shoulder to loosen knotting muscles and turned to stand behind her.

As he nuzzled her neck, she laughed. "I'm going to ruin this dinner."

"I don't care."

Smiling, she switched off the burner and angled her face up for a kiss. "If you get the beer, I'll bring the hamburgers—" His mouth silenced hers. Deepening the kiss, he offered her the gentleness no one else ever had, as if she were the most special woman in the world. Leigh held him tighter for a long moment. Only he could make her lungs ache from desire. Only he incited serenity with his tenderness. "After we eat," she said on a small sigh, "I thought we'd watch the scary late movie and—"

A slow smile curling his lips, he grazed her waist to rest his fingers on the sharp point of her hip. "And then?"

Delicately she ran a fingertip down his throat. "We'll think of something."

Leigh was never late for work. Running into the diner the next morning, she checked the clock on the wall behind the cash register and rounded the counter to start the coffee brewer. "'Morning."

A small frown marring her brow, Kathleen cast a sidelong glance while she counted out dollar bills and slipped them into a slot in the drawer of the cash register. "Are you going to want time off today?"

Leigh heard an angry edge in her sister's usually soft voice. "No."

"Good, because I don't want to have to handle the early dinner crowd by myself."

Leigh paused in scooping coffee grounds into the brewer basket. "I'll be here." Alert to the annoyance in her sister's voice, Leigh migrated closer and leaned forward to see Kathleen's face. "What's wrong?"

"Nothing."

"Why don't you look happy?"

She met Leigh with sad eyes. "Jim's restless. I know the signs. I've lived through them before. It's like what happened with Larry."

"That was different," Leigh reminded her.

"No, it wasn't. I can't go around pretending everything is wonderful. I did that before and made a fool of myself because I wouldn't admit that Larry and I didn't want the same thing anymore." She closed the cash register drawer harder than necessary. "Neither do Jim and I."

"Has he said something?"

"No," she flared, then released a huge sigh. "I'm sorry. I'm being a real witch."

Leigh touched her shoulder. "What can I do?"

Kathleen shook her head. "I don't think there's an answer to that. Nothing has been said, but I feel it. I feel the difference. Do you understand?"

Leigh did, only too well. Every smile, every touch, every kiss with Jake carried a message of love again.

Too quiet, Jake reflected while he drove her toward home that evening. She was too damn quiet. He knew this pondering side of her as well as the one when she laughed with delight over something silly. He knew enough to give her silence until she was ready to talk, to share. But because time together had been more than he'd hoped for, he couldn't quell an uneasiness now that she might be having regrets. And he couldn't stand the distance.

His eyes on the road, he inched his way through the invisible barrier. "We missed going to that movie last night. Do you want to go tonight?"

Staring out the window, she nodded. "Okay."

"Just okay?"

Leigh heard an unnatural doubt in his voice. "I'm sorry," she said on a soft laugh. "I was thinking about Kathleen."

Jake gave himself a mental kick. "Want to talk about it?"

"No. She wouldn't want me to."

"So, what movie?" Jake asked, not pressing her to divulge a confidence.

She shook off her frustration at her sister's dilemma, but it felt wrong that she could be so happy when Kathleen was miserable.

"Still thinking?"

Leigh snuggled closer and curled an arm around his neck. "Well, there's a heavy-duty foreign film—"

Jake groaned, stopping her.

"What about a thriller?"

"You're so subtle." He chuckled. "You wanted to go to that one, anyway, so why didn't you say so?"

"I was giving you a choice," she said, looking up from her purse when he parked in the driveway beside her house.

Turning off the engine, he sent her a you've-got-to-be-kidding look.

Leigh laughed, feeling young, feeling that all the years they'd lost had never happened. "It'll take me about ten minutes to get the smell of grease off me and change clothes."

Tugging her against his side, he climbed the steps with her. "I thought that you were trying out some new perfume."

"You have a mean streak," she reprimanded in a voice filled more with laughter than ire.

"Really mean," he said, amused, and stood back while she opened the door.

Stunned, Leigh scanned the room, which was over-flowing with daisies. They were everywhere—on the sofa, on the carpet, in vases around the room. She swung around to face him. "You're insane."

Grinning, he gathered her close. "They're a bribe."

Leigh raised a puzzled look at him. "For what?"

"There's a demolition derby next Thursday night."

With a laugh, she fell into his arms.

They had dinner at Barney's Pizza Palace in a neighboring town. The pizza proved better than the movie, a thriller about a roommate from hell.

"Ready for that ice cream now?" he asked, already drawing her across the street with him.

"I want—"

He tightened his grip on her hand. "A double scoop of chocolate peanut butter."

"You didn't forget."

"How could I?" He smiled in a wry, familiar way. "You liked the strangest things," he teased.

Affectionately she jabbed a finger at his chest. "No, you did. You're the guy who ate sardine sandwiches."

He curled his lips. "That's disgusting."

"I thought so, too. But I took the good with the bad," she teased, laughing and coiling her arms around his neck. She kissed his smiling lips lightly, then long and hard for no reason except she wanted to.

Drawing back slowly, she observed over his shoulder the stares of the two women coming out of the drugstore. Leigh nodded a greeting to Grace and Mrs. Melbourne, the pharmacist's wife. *I want them to see me with you,* she realized. *I want them to know that I never stopped loving you.* "Now where?" she asked.

Smiling, he kissed her nose. "The lake."

The lake. It was their special place, sheltered by trees and bushes. Leigh had used it as her thinking place, spending time alone there whenever the world had crashed down on her during the past ten years.

It was where she'd left her childhood behind her, where they'd made love for the first time. It was the one place she'd allowed herself to remember what had been and what might have been.

On her back, she closed her eyes and floated. She listened to Jake's steady splashing strokes growing louder as he swam closer to her. Then a hand, cool and wet, skimmed her thigh. With a toss of her head, the tips of her wet hair tickled the nape of her neck. "Were you trying to drown me?"

He yanked her closer, savoring the touch of her nipples hard against his chest. "Drown *in* you," he whispered hoarsely. Moonlight had teased him with glimpses of her pale skin while she'd swam, a hint of a thigh, a curve of her breast. Face-to-face with her now, their eyes meeting, he held her for a long moment, letting his free hand float over her slick softness.

Water slapping at his back, he closed his mouth over hers and searched, tasting the sweetness within while he trailed his fingers down her belly. She invited, enticed. Her hands played over him in a way so like before that he thought he'd go mad from the memory and the moment.

Clinging to him, she murmured softly against his mouth, encouraging him. Words weren't needed. The dark need, a pleasurable torment, closed in on him.

His mouth against her throat, he drifted, weightless though her arms and legs hugged him. He was a creature of his senses. Heat and moisture dominated everything, but he kissed her gently, seeking all she willingly offered. His fingers wound in her hair, and with a slowness that was almost reverent, he let the taste of her fill him. She was his. For this moment, she was his. That thought, more than desire, took his breath away.

They drifted until his feet touched bottom, the kiss deepening, wants blending with needs. His blood pounding, he didn't have the will to think. He was suddenly beyond anything but her skin shivering with his every caress. Breathless, he pulled her arching hips closer. For a second, he stilled, wanting to see her face again, see the heat of passion in her eyes. "I love you."

Emotion flooding her, she longed to give him everything, to tell him how she felt. If only for this moment, as every sound uttered, every caress, every beat of her heart was for him, she wanted him to know she was his. "I love you, too."

"Say it again," he demanded brokenly as he scrambled to check the rush of passion one more moment.

She drew a hard breath to answer him. "I love you."

Grasping on to reality for one second, he vowed to never let her take back those words.

Love. It bound them now with the same intensity that desire drove them. Her mouth found his again, more greedy, more insisting. The warmth of their breaths mingled as tongues met and dueled. And she ached, pleasure clouding her mind. Softly she murmured against his lips. She couldn't do more.

As her hands glided over him, he traveled through a misty fog. He was lost. He felt the coolness of the water around him, heard its gentle sound, but his mind centered on her, only her. His fingers entangling in her wet hair, he captured her breaths inside his mouth as they rose above the water, as the deep stirring ache soared through both of them. You are mine, he thought, feeling the pounding of her heart when she strained against him, opening herself, welcoming him. Then he drifted under, drowning beneath the waves of sensation.

Mindless, Leigh gazed at the needles of a pine tree shuddering beneath the night air. Her head on his chest, she traced the line of his jaw with a fingertip. She'd said the words, ones that she'd longed to say, ones that she'd locked inside her for ten years. Content, warmed by his body, she snuggled closer. "That was...wonderful."

The amazement in her voice pleased him. "You're beautiful," he whispered softly, stroking her hair. He

180 JAKE RYKER'S BACK IN TOWN

inhaled deeply, taking in her scent. The heat of her seeped through his senses. He could want her again. He'd had her taste, the feel of her around him, and he wanted more. It wasn't passion alone leading him. He longed for the closeness. With her in his arms, her heart pounding against him, he had no doubts.

Leigh angled her head to look up at him. Beneath the moonlight, the scar at his shoulder appeared whiter, jagged. Leigh stretched to kiss the spot. She wished for easy answers, for a way to accept everything he was as she had when she was seventeen. "How did this happen?"

He could sugarcoat the scene for her, but his life in the city wasn't honeyed with green trees and wildflowers. It was cement and grime and people who toted guns, who worried about the next fix or the next trick. "I was working undercover and trying to set up a drug buy. Someone remembered me from another bust. And all hell broke loose."

Though he'd spoken easily about it, her pulse hammered. She could visualize him staggering and pale.

"I didn't duck fast enough," he said lightly, shifting and drawing her under him so he could see her face. She'd never know the fears within him. He longed for only one thing—an acceptance by her of what he did, what they could have.

Leigh shook away the disturbing image and snaked an arm around his back. If she could, she'd wrap herself around him, keep him safe forever. "Slow reflexes," she teased deliberately, determined not to ruin the evening with her misgivings.

Jake didn't believe her smile, her airy response. "Want to test that?"

"Might as well." She turned her wet face up to him. "You know you've already sullied my reputation," she said on a soft laugh. "Have you heard we're the hot topic in town?"

He'd heard and it bothered him. He wasn't a cocky kid anymore, forging recklessly and impulsively after whatever he wanted without a care about consequences.

"We're having—" she paused for a dramatic gasp "—an affair."

Intimately he skimmed her hip with his hand. "That's the first time Grace Newell's been accurate in thirty years."

Leigh could have told him differently. Ten years ago, Grace had speculated that the child Leigh had carried belonged to Jake Ryker.

Propping himself on an elbow, he toyed distractedly with her hair and nudged back strands so he could nibble her ear. "Do you mind?"

"I'd mind more if it weren't true," she admitted on a sigh.

His hand at her hip again, he scooted down to press his mouth against her collarbone. "Want to go home?"

The quickened beat of his heart pounded in unison with hers. "Are you hinting about staying tonight?"

"Until Seaton is caught."

Leigh tightened her hold on him. "Oh, that's why you want to?" she murmured, but she was having trouble concentrating as he tauntingly ran a finger down to the dark shadow between her breasts. At his silence, she fought the dreamy sensation closing in on her from his caresses. "Or is there another reason?"

He wanted only to feel, to immerse himself in every detail of the moment. "Another reason."

"You're lucky you gave the right answer." Leigh shut her eyes. "Or we'd have had a fight."

With soft pale skin bewitching him, he slowly spread light kisses lower. "I don't want to fight."

Arching, Leigh pressed her head back. "I loved making up with you."

Lost in her scent, in the velvety texture of her, he could barely think. "Let's skip the preliminaries this time and go to the main event."

Chapter Eleven

A morning sky absent of sunshine carried the hint of more rain. Leigh, perched on the window seat that overlooked the woods, cradled a coffee cup. She'd allowed the passing days to seep into her mind like a keepsake. She wanted forever with him. She wanted it so badly that she ached. But she wanted him on her terms, not his. She couldn't stand the thought of another scar on his body from a bullet.

She couldn't imagine repeating the scene she'd endured nine years ago when she'd paced in a hospital waiting room. Ken had died immediately, but for three hours, her father had struggled for life. She'd waited in vain that time. If she had to live through that kind of moment for Jake, she'd die herself.

Coming in from outside, Jake wiped a rag across dirty fingers. The moment he saw her he forgot his irritation at the flat tire he'd changed. He could picture her like that, her face turned toward the light, a morning coffee cup in her hand. He didn't want that image to be only a memory. "Did you save me any coffee?"

Leigh swiveled a look at him. "There's a whole pot." As he crossed to the sink and lathered his hands, she could barely resist moving to him. She was becoming almost greedy to touch him, to feel the texture of his skin, his hair, to trace his features the way a blind person memorized. Fear was with her again, but it was a different kind as she allowed herself to consider even one day without seeing him.

His hands wet, he snagged a paper towel from the roll and turned in response to the ringing phone.

An unfamiliar voice answered Leigh's greeting. "Yes, he is." Leigh held the receiver out to him. "For you."

Jake balled the paper towel and aimed for the wastebasket with one hand while taking the receiver with his other. Though he'd given her number to Bob during their last conversation, he hadn't expected another call.

"Looking out for your best interests while you're away, I'm the bearer of good tidings," Bob said on a laugh. "Word came down yesterday. You got the promotion, Sarge. How's that for good news?"

"Terrific," he answered without much conviction. He felt nothing. He'd worked hard for this moment but... Gripping the receiver tighter, he shifted to watch Leigh leaving the room.

"Why do I get the feeling you aren't thrilled?"

"Sure I am." He didn't sound convincing even to himself. "More money. More authority."

"So when are you coming back? Don't you think it's time to get off of your lazy butt?"

Jake mumbled a response, a stall, not ready to walk away again.

For a few moments, Leigh idled away time in the living room, straightening magazines on the coffee table. When she strolled back into the kitchen, his back was to her.

Sensing her presence, he whipped around. "That was my partner."

Leigh darted an apprehensive glance at him. "Good news?"

"A promotion," he answered, filling his mug.

Her pulse slowed. The end was near, she knew. Everything would be over. The joy, the laughter, the love in her life. She strained for a smile. "That *is* good news."

"Detective Sergeant Ryker at your service," he said lightly, but the humor fell flat.

"Congratulations." With the same effort that she feigned enthusiasm, she made herself ask, "They want you back?"

It didn't soothe him that she could handle the idea so easily. "In a while." For a long moment, he stared out the window. Life threw some tough curves. What he'd wanted most was his now. Only it wasn't what he wanted most anymore. "We need to talk."

Not yet. She didn't want to talk, didn't want to think about the future, about a time without him. "Jake, not now," she appealed. "Let's not worry about anything right now."

He could have pressed her, but the edge of desperation in her voice stopped him. "That's the coward's way, Leigh."

"Be one with me for a little while," she said, slipping her arms around him and leaning close to press her cheek to his.

Dodging things wasn't his style, but the demand on the tip of his tongue remained there. He gathered her against him and closed his eyes. And he caught a glimpse of the future—without her.

He knew she loved him, but what if she couldn't get past her fear? That question plagued him later as he sat, leaning against a towering pine. The wind curling around him, he cast his fishing line in the water again. Whether she wanted to or not, he couldn't stop thinking about where they were going. The way he saw it, they were dancing around each other. The love and the laughter were back, but commitment eluded them.

He lit a cigarette and took a drag. She'd never pulled any punches about her feelings toward his job, and he didn't know anything else. His work had occupied lonely hours, had become such a part of him that even when he took off his badge and gun he was still a cop. But the promotion—something he'd worked hard for and held as his only goal weeks ago—suddenly meant nothing to him.

Not a smart way to think.

He'd grown up with good survival instincts; he'd had to. Giving up a job—every goal he'd ever had for the past ten years—made little sense. What future could he offer her as one of the unemployed?

If push came to shove, he wasn't even sure he could give up being a cop. Other than the Duke of Windsor, he knew of few men who'd given up everything for the woman they loved. It was a romantic gesture, but not practical. While he wouldn't be relinquishing a kingdom, he'd be shunning the life he'd made for himself during the past ten years, the only with any real future life he'd ever known.

But he wanted her. Hell, he throbbed for her. He had to believe she'd change her mind, that she wouldn't turn her back on him. They'd worked too hard to find each other again to simply go their separate ways.

Glancing at his wristwatch, Jake felt another tug on the line and stood to reel in the fish slowly.

"Got one?" It was Al, shuffling down the incline.

Without looking back at him, Jake answered, "Caught two so far."

"I'm kind of glad I ran into you." He shifted his stance to slouch against a tree. "We, uh, we need a third baseman for the game on Founder's Day. How about it?"

Amusement distracted Jake from the fish on his line. Police and media crowded the town because of

Seaton, but Pineview's deputy's biggest problem revolved around the absence of a third baseman.

Al scowled. "I see that smile," he admonished lightly. "This is serious. Our third baseman had to leave for Salt Lake because of business. We can't afford to forfeit this game. These guys have been ragging on us for months about how great they are and how they're going to get the division trophy and, well, you get the picture. You always were the best third baseman in town. Everyone always said so. So, will you help us?"

Jake grinned wryly, amazed how often he'd been hearing those words since he'd returned. More staggering was the news that there had been such praise for him. "Sure."

"Okeydokey."

Jake reeled in another fish. With tomorrow night's dinner caught, he strolled with Al back toward his Jeep. He had enough time to clean the fish and himself before he drove into town for his appointment with Wendley.

Playing the professional to the hilt, Wendley stood, offered a hand, then gestured toward a chair. As he tented his fingers in front of him on the desk, Jake recalled a fifth-grade teacher who'd had a propensity for the same annoying habit. Usually when he planned to scold.

"The price is fair," Wendley said in the pedantic tone of a man conveying *he* was the expert on such matters.

"I'm willing to sell everything but the land near the lake."

"You want more for it?"

Jake bent a leg and rested the heel of his boot on his knee. "No, it's not for sale." Disturbingly, he realized in that moment that he'd considered the possibility there might be no future for him and Leigh, but he wanted the lake there for her, a private place, a haven where she could go and think.

"I'm not sure they would be interested in the property without that part of it."

"That's their choice," he said, figuring the "they" Wendley had mentioned were the bank's stockholders.

Little was going as Leigh planned that day. She'd dealt with two surly customers, nearly brought Kathleen to tears by just mentioning Jim and learned her aunt hadn't returned home yet.

By midafternoon, she decided she'd waited long enough to handle Jake's problem. During her afternoon break, she dashed home and rushed into her father's study. Books lined a wall of shelves in the deep burgundy room. Trophies won for years in bow-and-arrow competitions gleamed behind the glass of an antique cabinet. Paintings of mallards adorned walls. He'd loved hunting. To her, it was less of a sport and more of a macho power trip. She'd always thought it a contradictory pastime for such a gentle man.

Leigh opened the top desk drawer and grabbed the ring of keys for the sheriff's office. Since the other night, when she'd learned what her father had done to Jake, she'd seen a different man, one who'd threatened Jake, who'd forced him to leave everything familiar. The image of that man knotted her stomach. She'd never stop loving her father, but in one night, years of respect had been whisked away.

His old man had had the last laugh, Jake mused. The town desperately wanted Ryker land to expand the recreation area. Jake jogged a path along Weaver Road. He could care less about the building or the land, except for the small part of the lake that was on Ryker property. That was his. The rest he'd willingly sell cheap.

Passing by his father's cottage, he groaned silently at the sight of an old neighbor, Elsie Kalesky. Loquacious as ever, she rambled on about everyone. Running in place, Jake listened, then moved backward, away from her. Turning around to follow a trail that paralleled the woods, he tucked a piece of her gossip into his mind.

His feet hitting the hard ground in a steady rhythm, he pushed himself at a faster pace than usual. By the time he returned to the motel, the sun had dropped behind the treetops.

Winded, he entered his motel room to the ringing of the telephone.

"Jake, it's me." The unsteadiness in Leigh's voice straightened him. Stretching the telephone cord, he reached for his shoulder holster. "I have the keys to the sheriff's office, to the file room."

He let his service revolver slip from his fingers back onto the chair. "When did you get them?"

"This afternoon."

"What do you mean, 'this afternoon'?" He didn't expect or wait for a response. "Dammit, Leigh. You're supposed to stay put."

"And you're supposed to say thank you instead of yelling at me."

He caught the edge of annoyance in her voice and hissed a soft breath. "Thank you." The words stuck in his throat as he visualized her running into Seaton while alone. "So Aunt Abby said yes?"

She acknowledged his softer tone, a signal that he wanted to calm the mood. "You know better than that. Anyway, she's still out of town. We could go tonight."

"I'll pick you up." Jake set down the receiver and wandered to the shower. Leaning back against a wall, he let the water spray over him. He should have been more grateful. He didn't need psychic power to know she'd struggled long and hard before taking such action. She was blatantly opposing her aunt. It seemed that the young innocent girl who used to bend over backward to please her family had changed. People associated heroism with brave acts. He saw it in a slim redhead.

Leigh expected he'd be in a grumpy mood. While she didn't feel she was in danger in the middle of the day, especially with so many people in town preparing for Founder's Day, she believed in caution. She'd watched for cars trailing her, had even withdrawn a can of Mace from her purse before getting out of her car, and had checked the back seat before getting back in. She doubted Jake would be interested in hearing any of that.

In her uncle's office, she changed into the clothes she'd brought back with her from the house. Dressed in jeans, a black pullover and dark sneakers, she bounded out of the diner at eight that night.

Before she even slammed shut the Jeep door, Jake proved predictable. "Don't go wandering off like that again."

Leigh debated with herself. Though annoyed by his attitude, she comprehended that a lot of caring and worrying was behind his disagreeableness.

"Did anyone know you were going home? Did you see anything suspicious? Where did you get the keys?"

Slowly Leigh counted to five, then answered calmly, "I told Kathleen. I saw nothing, not even Eddie, though I hit seventy at the edge of town."

"*You* were speeding?"

"I wanted to get back fast," she said, setting her shoulder bag on the floor.

His arm on the ledge of the car's opened window, Jake eased onto Main Street. "Before I knew you'd left."

Sensing the start of argument two, Leigh sidetracked him by asking, "Aren't you hungry?"

His glare softened. "You haven't eaten?"

"Does a candy bar count?"

He negotiated the Jeep into a fast-food drive-in where they used to eat every Friday night after a football or basketball game. "Hamburger with double onions? And a double chocolate shake?"

A giggle bubbled in her throat. "You remember?"

"Everything." She was making it easy for them. Wanting to avoid any more harsh words, he decided to change the mood. "There isn't any woman except you that I'd spend a Saturday afternoon with, watching a marathon of Cary Grant movies."

"I deserved it after you made me spend an evening digging up worms for fishing."

His laugh drifted over her. "Classy and romantic, wasn't I?"

Her voice softened with affection. "I thought so."

"You were young, inexperienced," he gibed lightly before leaving the car to get their orders.

She could have told him of all the others who'd said the same thing to dissuade her from him. Being young hadn't kept her from knowing her own heart.

A bag dangling from his hand, he slid back in behind the steering wheel and handed her the food before turning on the engine. Leigh dug in and retrieved a hamburger for him. "Hamil came in the diner today," she said between bites of her sandwich. "And I heard that they're going to do a house-to-house search." Distress wrinkled her brow. "For some reason, they changed their minds. Now they think Seaton's holed up around here."

"So do I." He watched her smother her fries with catsup. "About earlier today," he started, then stopped. He'd been furious with her for taking any chances.

"You already thanked me."

"Grudgingly," he admitted.

Leigh offered him a french fry. "I know."

Jake took the soggy fry as if it were a peace pipe. "Where did you get the keys?"

"From my father's desk at home." Leigh slurped her drink. "I remember my father kept an extra set of keys because Al always locked them in the office."

A quietness prevailed on Main Street. Jake parked in front of Melbourne's Drugs and finished his hamburger and soda. Like the other storefronts, Melbourne's was dark, but a light shone in the sheriff's office. "What we're going to do is illegal," he reminded her. "You know that, don't you?"

Leigh finished chewing. "I think it's more criminal not to give the report to you."

Amused, he laughed. "Remember that if we end up sitting in a cell."

She set down her drink and hunched close to the dashboard to peer out the window. "Al or Eddie must still be there. We'll have to wait."

To avoid arguing, he refrained from telling her that she wasn't going in with him. "I caught dinner for tomorrow," he said instead. "Three trout of respectable size," he added with a prideful grin.

"You went fishing today?" She wiped her hands with a napkin and set it and their cups back in the bag.

"And I aggravated your friend Wendley."

As he relayed his conversation with Mark, Leigh inclined her head quizzically. "Why didn't you sell all of the property?"

"It seemed a sacrilege to give up the lake property to someone else." Turning toward her, he stroked a finger along the curve of her jaw. "Want to neck?"

Leigh stifled a smile. "Aren't you too old for back-seat grappling?"

He gave her an affronted look. "Grappling? I thought I was smooth."

A laugh flowed up from her throat. "Really smooth," she said as he curled a hand around her shoulder and tugged her toward him exaggeratedly and clumsily.

"You haven't seen anything yet."

His hand beneath her shirt ignited a small fire inside her. Leigh smiled against his cheek. "Guess you've improved." Nearly sighing, she arched away from the moist heat of his mouth on her neck. "We have to stop." She laughed again. "You're getting hot and bothered."

"Glad you noticed."

"Jake?"

"Now what?"

Over his shoulder, she saw a light go out in the sheriff's office. "He's leaving," she said as Eddie strolled out the door, locked it and headed down the street, probably to make his nightly rounds. "Coast is clear."

He smoothed down her T-shirt. "You watch too many movies with B dialogue."

"You got me addicted to them," she reminded him before opening her door and sliding out of the Jeep. Leigh met him on the sidewalk.

Together, they scurried down the dark alley behind the building. Next door, the Doberman in the yard behind the hardware store barked zealously.

"Shh." Leigh crossed and made her way to the fence.

"Get away from him," Jake scolded in a whisper.

"Quit yelling. You'll upset him."

"Upset him? He sounds ready to charge through the fence."

Leigh crept closer. "Hercules, shh."

Jake squinted an eye at her. "Hercules?"

Through a separation in the fencing, she touched the dark, wet nose. "Be quiet, sweet boy. It's okay." Leigh fished in the pocket of her jeans and withdrew a beef jerky, then slipped it between the boards.

"Some watchdog," Jake mumbled.

"He's very particular. He wouldn't take something from just anyone." Her voice trailed off as he held his palm out to her.

"Give me the keys. You can stay here and keep him calm. Be the lookout."

Leigh recoiled from his reach. "I'm going in."

In the darkness, their eyes locked challengingly.

"We don't have time for this."

She matched his impatient tone. "Then let's not make a big deal out of it. I *am* going in."

He snatched her wrist before she could take a step around him and effectively trapped her between him and the building. "Whether you have the keys or not, this could be viewed as breaking and entering," he said low, their lips nearly touching. "We don't have any right to go in there."

Holding steady, Leigh insisted. "I go in with you or you don't get these keys."

When she was sparked, her stubbornness was unequaled. He mumbled a choice word that Leigh chose to ignore. "All right."

Leigh tossed him the keys, then aimed the flashlight over his arm at the lock. "This is kind of exciting."

"Thrilling."

Overlooking his testy tone, she placed a hand on his back and copied his steps into the dark room. Single file, they inched their way past the two empty cells and turned left, passing the bathroom.

Jake unlocked the storage room door and fanned the beam from the flashlight around the small rectangular room and the stacks of cartons piled three-high along the wall. Creeping forward, Leigh bent over to read the label on one carton. "Do you want—?" With a look back, she noted he was aiming the light at her bent backside. "What are you doing?"

He flashed a smile. "Taking advantage of an opportunity."

"Let's get serious here." Frowning, she beamed the light at her wristwatch. "How long do you think we have before Eddie comes back?" she asked in her best down-to-business tone.

"Depends on how slow he walks."

"He usually gets sidetracked when he passes Sallie's Beauty Salon."

Close to him, she caught Jake's amused grin.

"You start at that end," he said, pointing.

For the next half hour, they worked in silence, opening cartons, shooting their flashlights into them and reading the names on the manila folders.

Sitting on a dusty carton, Jake dug out a file.

Leigh kneaded the tightening muscle of one shoulder. "I don't think I'm going to find anything down here," she said quietly. "Most of these reports were written by Sheriff Carlson. Remember him?"

Vaguely, Jake thought. He remembered the portly man looking for his father because someone had filed a charge against him for starting a fight in one of the taverns near the lake. At nine, Jake knew his old man had been guilty. In his youth, Leonard Ryker had been a hell-raiser, a skirt-chaser who thought he couldn't be refused by any woman. Jake's only thought had been that he was glad his mother hadn't been alive, sharing his shame.

"Do you remember Sheriff Carlson?" Leigh repeated, but moved closer and, curious, craned her neck to read the name on the file in his hands. "'Ryker, Jake.'"

"My past is haunting me." His lips curved into a boyish smile. "I can't believe what I got into." A lot of mischief. He'd thought he was tough in those days. Since then, he'd seen a lot of kids in trouble. Like him, they wore a mask to hide the hurt.

"You—" Leigh caught her breath at the sound of footsteps coming down the hall toward the bathroom. "Eddie's back," she whispered. She flicked off her flashlight in unison with Jake.

In the dark, he yanked her close against him. The door creaked open, and light from the hallway shone on them.

Staring at Al, Leigh hoped they didn't look as guilty as she felt. "We're busted," she mumbled out of the corner of her mouth to Jake.

"Find anything?" Al drawled from the doorway, flicking up the light switch.

Though Leigh doubted Al would escort them to a cell, she stirred up her most innocent smile. "Are you going to throw us out?"

"I didn't let you in. Why would I throw you out?" He shrugged a meaty shoulder. "But if anyone asks, remember I didn't give you the keys." He surveyed the opened boxes. "We've been keeping an eye on Seaton's sister, like you suggested. Eddie said she's been staying close to home."

Jake released his protective grip on Leigh's waist. "There might be someone else to watch."

Resuming her search, Leigh thumbed through the files and listened absently to their conversation.

"Who's Emmy Phillips?" Jake asked.

Leigh shot an astonished look up at him. "The librarian's daughter?"

"Seaton was hot for her."

Leigh's eyes rounded. "What!"

Al swung around. "You're kidding me."

"Who said?" Leigh questioned.

"Elsie Kalesky." Jake slanted her a grin. "Weaver Road's Grace Newell."

"I'll be damned." Al looked ready to explode. "Wouldn't that be something?" he said, beaming. "What if she's the one who's hiding him or knows where he's at? What if Eddie and me found him? That'd be something, wouldn't it? That would sure make this town sit up and take notice," he said, turning away and leaving, his fantasy blooming.

Leaning forward, Leigh flipped open carton flaps. "It would be good for them. No one thinks they know what they're doing. They're not really trained to be in charge."

Considering the pressure both men were under, Jake thought they were handling themselves well. "They seem to be doing okay," he said, lifting down another carton.

At the other end of the room, Leigh struggled with a box. She wondered if they'd even find what they were looking for. "Jake, I can't believe how much is in these boxes. I have—"

Head bent, he was hunkering before a carton.

"Find a centerfold?" she teased. As he slowly raised his eyes to her, nerves jumped inside her.

"Here."

Leigh shook her head at the paper and drew back as if evil were lunging for her. "Tell me."

"He wasn't guilty. Someone else confessed."

Leigh nearly stumbled over a box to get to him. "Who?"

"A transient named Elliot Kimball."

Her spine stiffened at the implications of his words.

In a dead tone, he read her father's scrawled writing. "'Kimball died in an Ogden hospital of burns days after the fire.'"

In disbelief, she dropped to carton and hunched forward. "He confessed?"

"That's what your father wrote."

Leigh took a deep, long breath. It didn't calm her, didn't slow down the quickness of her pulse. "Go on. What else?"

"He had a rap sheet."

"For?"

"Arson."

He had to be wrong. She studied his face a moment, then snatched the report from him. "Why wasn't any of this made public?"

He heard the choked sound in her voice, but couldn't wrestle with both his emotions and hers at the moment. Bitterness edged his voice. "Yeah, why wasn't it?"

Stunned, Leigh deliberated over the report written by her father. Why hadn't he cleared Leonard Ryker? Why had her father allowed suspicions to fester against him?

Chapter Twelve

For Leigh, nothing would be the same again. She'd taken the keys, not thinking she and Jake would learn anything that wasn't already known. She'd always thought that whatever her father had told her was law. She'd truly believed he could do no wrong. Well, he could; he had.

During the drive back to her house, Jake dealt with his own feelings. He'd wanted the truth. Now that he had it, he wasn't sure what to do with it. He only knew he'd taken something from the one person in his life he'd never wanted to harm.

"I don't understand," she murmured when they reached her porch.

A curse rose in his throat—at himself as much as her father—as she turned eyes desperate for a logical answer on him. He had his truth now, but wondered if it had been worth what he'd done to her.

"Leigh, I'm sorry." How could he explain that her pain hurt more than every slur, every suspicious look he'd endured because his name was Ryker?

"You're sorry?"

"For what you're feeling."

"There has to be a reason." She yearned for an explanation, longed for some kind of rationalization about what her father had done. He wasn't a dishonest man, yet he'd taken an oath about justice and had turned his back on it.

The eyes meeting his were filled with disbelief. "Maybe it was enough that he didn't like him."

"No." Leigh shook her head.

He'd witnessed this fight within her before. She was battling for strength to keep from bursting into tears.

"That's not enough," she said, sounding stronger, calmer. She had to find out, Leigh realized. A feud between his family and hers had begun at some time. She needed to know why. One person could give her the answers—her aunt.

The next day, Leigh repeatedly called her aunt's home. At five-thirty, the maid provided the response she'd been waiting for.

"Mrs. Martin arrived home an hour ago."

Impatient, Leigh almost left on her own. The moment Jake pulled up to the curb in front of the diner, she scurried out to him. "Aunt Abby is back," she said even before she'd closed the door behind her.

Unable to shake the image of her pale face while she'd read the report, Jake thought she needed a reminder. "You don't have to see her."

That would be the easy way, Leigh mused. "But I do. I need to know why all of that happened."

Jake switched on the windshield wipers as rain fell in fat, quick drops. "You really expect her to tell you about some feud?"

"I'm not leaving until she does."

Some of the hardest moments required nothing more than taking the first step, Leigh reminded herself as she followed the maid down the elegant hallway to her aunt's study.

"I'm so glad you came," her aunt greeted warmly. "I had a wonderful time visiting the Rossiters. Do you remember them?"

"Yes. Yes, I do." Leigh's footsteps echoed in the high-ceilinged room.

"Tea?" she asked, reaching for the silver server.

"I'd like that." Her stomach fluttering, Leigh perched on the pale blue brocade settee.

"Mrs. Rossiter's son is as obnoxious as ever."

She went on, but Leigh listened distractedly, nodding agreeably and waiting for her to end her recap of her Tucson visit. "Aunt Abby, I need to talk to you about something," she said, accepting the teacup.

"This sounds rather serious."

Leigh remained steady beneath her watchful gaze. "I'd like to know why our family was always against the Rykers."

"Is *that* what you consider so important?"

"It *is* important," Leigh insisted.

The slim smile on her aunt's face faded. "I'm amazed. When you were a child, I expected him to have this awful influence on you. But you're a woman now."

"Why did you expect that then?"

"For obvious reasons," she said in a tone that indicated she thought Leigh obtuse for asking. "He was wild."

"He isn't now," Leigh returned. "Yet you still don't like him."

"It's enough to say he's like his father."

"He's not like his father. He's a responsible, honest man. He always has been."

Her aunt's head reared back. "Just as I thought. You are in love with him again," she said with a disdain that made the idea sound criminal. "You're as foolish as the rest in this town."

Puzzled, Leigh set down the cup in her hand. "What about the rest?"

"Idiots. They're all idiots, including Tebner. Imagine even suggesting a Ryker for sheriff."

The announcement rocked Leigh as she visualized Jake in the uniform that her father had worn. As quickly as the image formed, she banished it. Her aunt would never allow it, and Jake wouldn't accept. He had a life elsewhere, a promotion waiting for him. "People realize he's a good man," she said in his defense. "Everyone else can see that. Why can't you? Why are you so against him? What made you and my father do what you did?"

Her aunt bristled. "I beg your pardon?"

"I've read the report about the fire."

"You read it? Did Deavers give—"

Leigh shook her head. "No, Al didn't."

"Then Jake Ryker must have broken into the office," she said in a slow manner, a small smile of satisfaction curving her thin lips. "Well, *he's* hardly the law-abiding citizen everyone is suddenly convinced he is." Even before she finished, her hand had closed over the telephone receiver.

"What are you going to do?"

"Have him arrested. He obtained that report by—"

"Before you make that call, let me tell you. I gave him the keys. I broke in with him. So if he's arrested, so am I. That wouldn't look too good, would it? A niece of a Martin arrested."

Her aunt's face paled. "What has come over you?"

"The truth," Leigh said firmly, bolting to a stand. "Aunt Abby, I've learned a lot, a lot I'm not proud about. What I want to know is why." At her aunt's silence, she warned, "If you don't tell me, then Uncle Matt will—"

"He doesn't know. He was away in the service. He never knew any of this."

Leigh abandoned the bluff and appealed. "Aunt Abby, please. Jake deserves to know more. He's helped around here. At the accident, in the search for Randy Seaton, he's proven that he's not like his father. Why did my family hate the Rykers so much that they were willing to let an innocent man go to jail for something he didn't do?"

"Innocent!"

"He was. He didn't start the fire. He wasn't treated fairly."

"Oh, you're so certain of that, aren't you?"

"No. I'm certain of nothing except he wasn't guilty of starting that fire." Leigh stared at her angry eyes. "The least we can do is be fair to his son and tell him why that happened."

Her aunt's back stiffened. "Fairness," she quipped. "How easily you throw that word around. Fairness is deserved. Your father was only making him understand that."

Bewildered, Leigh remained silent.

"And he tried to protect you, too. Jake Ryker is like his father. He, too, was exciting—and evil."

Her stomach queasy, Leigh dropped to the chair closest to her.

Jake peered through the rain-splattered car window at her, huddled in her Windbreaker, sidestepping puddles. Behind a sheet of rain, the giant house was lost to him.

As she opened the door, the Jeep's inside light caught her face. Wet and pale, she tugged the door closed. "She told me," she said softly. "She finally told me."

Jake draped an arm on the seat behind her and leaned closer.

"She was young, defiant." Despite Leigh's efforts to remain calm, her voice lowered with emotion. "You know how strong willed she is," she added, praying he'd feel the same understanding that had enveloped her. "When she wants something, no one stops her.

There was a carnival in the next town. She and a few girlfriends went there without permission. When they were coming home, a car stopped, and the driver asked if they wanted a ride. They had no reason to refuse. They knew Leonard Ryker. He went to the same school.''

Jake watched her face closely as lightning played over it for a second. He felt his insides knot. She was avoiding his eyes. Why? Why wouldn't she look at him?

''He took the other girls home. But she was Abigail McCall. And I imagine even as a young girl my aunt believed she was better than others. He didn't take her home.''

Leigh doubted she'd ever forget the strain in her aunt's voice that had communicated decades of sorrow. ''He drove into the woods.'' She warred with herself to get out the words. ''And he raped her.''

''Raped?'' The word came out as if it were foreign and he was trying to understand its meaning. ''He raped her?''

She wanted to help, but what comfort could she offer? ''They never charged him with it.''

''Why the hell didn't they?''

''Times were different back then.'' She felt as inept with him as she had with her aunt. Taking a deep breath, she gathered strength to tell him everything. ''There weren't any rape counselors, or anyone to assure the victim that she'd done nothing wrong. She felt shame. She didn't want others to know what happened. So he was never punished for it.''

Leigh touched his hand on the steering wheel. "My father and grandfather were the only ones who knew about it. When she realized she was pregnant, my grandfather sent her away, so no one knew but the family."

He looked away, hating the blood that linked him to his father.

The look on his face tugged at her heart. Sympathy rose in Leigh. She knew better than to offer it. Instead, she tightened her hand over his. "I can imagine what she went through. She was a child, barely sixteen. She must have been terribly ashamed." Leigh quieted for a moment and listened to the crickets. The moon slanted light into the woods, revealing gnarled tree branches. She couldn't recall her aunt ever going into those woods. "Revenge was all they cared about," Leigh said softly. "My grandfather convinced the sheriff then that his car had been stolen."

"And framed my old man?"

"Yes." The admission made her ill. Sharp, conflicting emotions were smothering her—sympathy for her aunt and for Jake rivaled a deep shame at her family's actions. "That's what he was sent to prison for, but you told me they paroled him early. All those years, the anger never went away. When my father became sheriff, he had more control."

Jake knew there was no easy way to ask the next question. "And the child?"

"She wouldn't talk about it." Leigh slid across the seat closer to him. "She only said that after she had it, they took it away from her." At his silence, she peered at him in the dark car.

Eyes straight ahead, he dealt with the anger bubbling inside him. "He deserved worse than he got. A damn lot worse." His gaze locked with hers. "He never cared about or loved anyone, Leigh."

She'd always believed that about her aunt. A marriage for money and no children had seemed so calculating. But she'd suffered, Leigh mused. She'd truly suffered. "My aunt's a proud woman. Neither she nor my father ever forgot what he did to her."

"Which is why they never trusted me with you."

Quiet, Leigh stared out the window. She understood now why her father had turned his back on a sworn oath. That didn't excuse his actions, but his love for his sister had been strong. At some point, they must have felt they had no other choice. Leigh could understand what he'd done to Leonard but not to Jake. She could empathize with her aunt's anguish and the bitterness that had gnawed at her for years. But so much harm had been done because of hatred and vengeance. And Jake had deserved none of it.

He lit a cigarette. He had the truth now. That's what he'd come back for. He'd changed since that rainy night when he'd driven into town. He'd been festering with resentments then—at the town, at the injustice against his father, at Leigh. Now, he felt shame and anger. It was directed at one man. His father, more than anyone else, had stolen everything from him and Leigh.

Over morning coffee, Leigh had watched him brood over what they'd learned last night. While she believed there were times when a person was entitled to such moments, she knew Jake well enough to guess he was sharing some unnecessary guilt. The weather wasn't helping his mood, it was dismal. Off and on, drizzling rain dotted the window of the Jeep as they drove toward town.

"I'll have to meet you at the baseball field," she said to draw him out of his mood.

"I don't know why I'm doing that."

"Because you're a big show-off," she teased.

"A show-off?"

Leigh laughed at the trace of indignation in his voice. "The biggest."

"Maybe it'll be canceled."

She knew differently. Though the gray morning threatened to ruin the town's Founder's Day celebration, Pineview residents were a determined lot. Even if it stormed, they'd cheer for the parade, grab thrills on the rides at the midway and stuff themselves with hot dogs and cotton candy. Somehow they'd ignore the gloomy weather and the hordes of law-enforcement men and the reporters hanging around town because of Seaton.

Jake wondered why he'd agreed to play the game. Even it would revive a difficult memory. He'd been playing in it his eighteenth year and drawing cheers when his father had shown up, drunk. He'd cussed out several people and had thrown an ineffectual punch at someone before he'd finally left.

Leigh noted the distant look in Jake's eyes. He was thinking back. She knew to which day. As if it were yesterday, she recalled the humiliation in Jake's eyes after the episode with his father. "They need you," she said as encouragement.

He made a skeptical face.

"Would you believe *I* need you?"

Braking, he released a short, quick laugh. "Yeah, you're a sucker for show-offs."

"Only a certain one," she murmured against his mouth, taking a quick kiss before she ventured through the rain to the diner.

Jake sat in his car for a long moment and scanned Main Street. The emotion playing through him eased off. For too long, he'd wondered how much he was like his old man. No more proof was needed. Because of his job, violence sometimes entered his life, but it wasn't a part of him. He carried the name Ryker, but was nothing like the man who'd strode around town drunk, who'd looked for a fight at the slightest provocation, who'd done the unthinkable to one woman.

There was little he could do to change the past, but the future promised more than he'd hoped for, if he could convince Leigh of what he'd always known—they were meant for each other. A damn big if.

By nature, he was logical, almost to a fault. But hard as he tried, he couldn't think of a reasonable argument to erase the one and only obstacle that might still steal happiness from them.

In a restless mood, he returned to his motel room and collected a few clothes and his carryall bag. At her house again, he finished packing. That's all he did. This time, he'd decide when he would leave. The big question was, would she be with him?

Desperate for a diversion from his own thoughts, he shoved the packed bag into the closet and drove toward the high school gymnasium.

The voices of fitness addicts echoed from the basketball court to the weight-lifting room. Jake lifted weights for half an hour, then spent the next two hours on the racquetball court with Don.

Though tired and sweaty, Jake felt better. The fatigue helped alleviate some of the last lingering traces of anger.

"I've had it," Don yelled, perspiration dripping down his face.

Jake smiled. "It was your idea to keep going."

"Been eating out too much." He patted a hand at a rock-hard stomach. "If you're looking for a different place to eat, I discovered a Vietnamese restaurant about forty-five minutes from here."

"Who's the lady in your life?" Jake asked as they ambled toward the showers.

Don blotted a towel at his forehead. "A schoolteacher from another town."

That he hadn't named her didn't offend Jake. In small towns, you kept your business to yourself or everyone knew it.

Don dropped the used towel into a wire basket they passed. "It's good to be dating again. Emmy Phillips and I were an item for a while, but that ended. I was kind of glad when she broke things off."

Interested, Jake slowed his stride. "She lives near Acorn Drive, doesn't she?"

"That's Emmy's mother's house."

"She doesn't live there, too?"

"Oh, sure. Her mother watches her like a hawk. We met a few times to be alone, but I figured if a thirty-one-year-old woman has to sneak out, then something isn't right."

"Where did you two meet?" Jake asked curiously.

"Hey." His voice colored with disappointment. "You know me better than that. I don't kiss and tell."

Jake mouthed an explicit curse that stirred Don's laugh. "I'm not asking for the name of the motel."

"Why are you asking *any* of this?" Don grinned crookedly. "The only female you ever looked at was Leigh. That hasn't changed, has it?"

Jake spun the lock on the metal cabinet. "No, that hasn't changed."

"So why?"

"Someone mentioned her name and Seaton's in the same breath."

"That's trouble." He plopped down on the bench and gave his head a slow shake. "Dumb, Emmy. Really dumb," he said as if she were near.

"Where?" Jake asked in the insistent tone he'd used successfully during interrogations.

"There's a spot out past Janzer's Ranch. Quiet, secluded. An abandoned mining shack hidden by overgrown shrubs. Hell, we were there when old man Janzer rode by on his horse, and he never saw us. Most people don't even know it exists."

It sounded to Jake like a perfect place to hide.

Chapter Thirteen

Jake showered, then hustled into his clothes. Within ten minutes, he was driving back toward Main Street. Sunshine peeked from behind fast-moving clouds. Grumblingly he accepted his fate for the day; he was going to play ball with the Pineview Pirates.

Zipping into the parking lot adjacent to the sheriff's office, he spotted Al standing with Hamil, head of the task force. Hamil sported a blue suit as immaculately cut as his white hair.

With Jake's approach, Hamil swung a sharp-eyed stare on him. Jake sensed no welcome sign. "Has there been a search of Janzer's property yet?"

Hamil cocked his head. "Where is that?"

Al rattled off directions.

Staring at the woods as if visualizing the place, he offered Jake an indifferent look. "We combed that area already."

Jake lounged against the black mobile command unit. "Wouldn't hurt to try again," he suggested, knowing to tread lightly. This man had the authority here, not him. "I learned there's a dilapidated mining shack hidden by brush on the property."

Hamil didn't respond with any interest, but pointed at Al. "You can check there if you want."

"I will," Al assured him. "Later tonight." When Hamil walked away, he muttered an expletive. "They act like we haven't any brains."

Jake smiled. "What do you care what they think about you? What you know about yourself is what's important." It was a code he'd lived by most of his youth.

Al gave him a wide grin. "Thanks. I needed that." He switched their conversation to the day's big softball game. "If you wait a minute, I'll get your shirt and cap."

Hours later, decked out in a T-shirt and cap that proudly announced he belonged to the Pineview Pirates, Jake wondered what he was doing. Ten years ago, he'd tried his damnedest to belong to this town. He'd played sports through school, he'd volunteered at the fire department to dispel everyone's notion that the name Ryker spelled trouble.

People had pretended. They'd smiled and talked to him, congratulated him when he'd achieved some thrilling feat on the playing field, but the moment something had gone wrong, all eyes had turned in his or his father's direction. He knew now how much they'd all been programmed to think that way under the influence of Sheriff McCall and Abby Martin. He knew now how much his father had deserved their hate.

Though his father and Hal McCall were gone, not much had really changed. If he hadn't had a badge to flash when he'd come back, no one would have trusted him to walk their dog. He didn't belong here, he reminded himself. He had a job in the city, a few friends, and acquaintances who knew he was one of the good guys. Here, he was still that Ryker kid from the other side of Weaver Road who hadn't been good enough for the sheriff's daughter.

As someone cleared their throat, Jake raised his eyes from the dirt he'd been pushing around with the toe of his cleats.

Donning a pale blue polo shirt and white pants, Wendley looked more suited for a yacht club celebration than a baseball game. Dust swirled in the air. Squinting, he turned an annoyed expression on Jake. "I came to tell you that the bank would like to purchase your property. They're agreeable to your stipulation that the lake parcel not be included. We could meet at the bank tomorrow morning to finalize the transaction."

Jake gave a nod. His old man was probably turning over in his grave. All those years with nothing. He'd been sitting on a gold mine and hadn't realized it.

* * *

"Are you my designated bodyguard?" Leigh asked
while strolling with Eddie toward the softball field.
He'd already informed her that Jake had refused to
play until Al promised that one of them would escort
her.

"Best duty I've had since coming here."

Leigh smiled. "Smooth tongue, Eddie."

He laughed and blushed slightly.

From blocks away, the dazzling lights and music of
the carnival drifted on the muggy wind. The smell of
grease from the concession stands clung to the air. The
town hall was decorated in red, white and blue. At the
center of town, the women's horticultural club had
done Pineview proud with a display of roses around
the gazebo. Celebration filled the air. Kids slurped ice-
cream cones, teenagers filed in line for a thrill on the
newest midway ride, older residents gathered around
different tables, playing bingo or reminiscing about
past Founder's Days.

With a wave to Kathleen on a bleacher, Leigh
weaved her way toward her.

"We were losing until the seventh inning," Lester
Newell told her.

"Then Jake hit one clear over to the next county,"
Clyde Banner added.

Amused by his exaggeration, Leigh inched past him.

"Smacked that ball out of the field and into the
parking lot of the lumber mill with three men on,"
Doc Higley informed her.

Smiling, Leigh plopped down beside Kathleen.
"We're down one?"

"Not for long." Kathleen motioned with her head toward Jake, who was stepping into the batter's box.

The runners on first and third tauntingly danced away from their bases. The pitcher threw a quick ball to first base, but the runner skidded back on his stomach and fingertipped the bag for a "safe" call.

Jake practiced several swings, then planted his feet and played a visual duel with the pitcher. The ball whizzed over home plate, and the crowd groaned with the umpire's first strike call. Shouts of encouragement from the stands followed strike two. Leigh straightened, curling her hand so tightly her nails bit into her flesh.

"Make it a good one, Jake," Kathleen bellowed.

The opposing team's pitcher wound up, then released a fastball.

"Big mistake," Leigh announced with delight, almost in unison with the *swoosh* of the bat.

The ball rocketed through center field and over the lights. Excitement electrified the air as Jake jogged around the bases. Standing, the crowd welcomed him back to home plate with ear-piercing screams and whistles. He trotted toward the dugout, but got only halfway. Teammates rushed out and leapt at him. The cheers that surrounded Leigh punctuated the pounding of her heart.

Welcome home, Jake, Leigh mused.

"You sure were one fine ballplayer years back," Lester Newell said as Jake made his way into the dugout to change out of his cleats.

His fingers hooked on the dugout fence, Clyde Banner snorted. "What happened in the past don't count." He gave Jake a broad grin. "Now's important. You're still one hell of one now."

Amused, Jake responded with a thank-you nod and squeezed past teammates and well-wishers to join Leigh near the gates. "How did I do, coach?"

Leigh rocked her hand in a so-so gesture.

He plopped his cap on her head. "You're tough to please." There was probably more truth in his words than either of them wanted to admit.

"I've seen better plays," she teased.

His brows lowered as he feigned a threatening look. "Like what?"

"Well..." Slipping her hand in his, she gazed up at the sky as if an answer might be there. "The Willie Mays catch over his shoulder."

Jake groaned. "Come on, give me some slack."

Leigh laughed. "Okay, tell me." Looking up, she felt a drop of rain plop on the bridge of her nose. "What's the most winning play?"

"That's easy to answer." His eyes sparkled with humor. "Eleven years ago, Marcie Webler going at it with that carnival guy behind the snack shack." As she rolled her eyes, he laughed and tugged her toward the Jeep. They reached it a second before the rain began to really fall.

Raindrops plopped in a steady, syncopated beat. Jake swore as the tires of his car slid on the slick road. He made a cautious turn into her driveway and glanced at Leigh. Despite the harrowing drive, she

looked calm. She was a strong woman, far more resil-
ient than she believed.

He flicked off the engine and touched her arm to
stop her from reaching for the door handle. For longer
than he'd wanted, he'd avoided this moment. He
needed words of commitment. He needed to know she
was really his.

Leigh turned a smile on him. "Don't tell me you
want to neck here when a bed is so close?"

Her teasing didn't reach him. "I want to talk."
Facing her, he draped an arm on the seat back. "I believe everything that happened doesn't matter. Only
now counts. Leigh, I love you. I want to marry you."

Her smiled faded. "Jake, I—"

"You said you loved me. Do you?" he asked before she could argue differently.

She listened to the rain pelting at the roof of the
Jeep, its quick beat matching the rhythm of her heart.
There would never be anyone else for her. Didn't he
realize that? "You know I do."

That was enough for him. Whatever problems they
faced, they could handle, he assured himself. "Then
nothing else does matter," he whispered, drawing her
closer.

She did love him, but... She stopped the thought.
"No, nothing else matters." In his arms, with his
mouth on hers, she believed him. She clung, her lips
answering his. Achingly she wanted to take another
chance. For him, she had to.

Almost punishingly, the rain whipped at them as
they scrambled up her porch steps. A flash of light-

ning threatened, cracking across the sky. Though drenched, she looked beautiful, her hair curling in whatever direction it wanted, moisture sparkling on her lashes. Too tempted not to, he pushed back strands of her wet hair and kissed the curve of her neck.

"I can't concentrate when you do that," she said with a laugh, fumbling to slip the key into the lock. "And you want to get out of these wet clothes, don't you?"

"Give me the keys."

Giggling at his eager tone, she opened the door. But the moment she flicked on the light switch, she froze.

Jake banged into her. "What are you—?"

She swayed back against him.

Unsure if she was ill, he caught her at the waist. It took only a second. Even before he stepped around her, he smelled the smoke. From an ashtray on the coffee table, a cigarette smoldered. Near it lay a half-eaten apple.

Leigh heaved a deep breath. "Someone broke in." Her voice sounded strange to her own ears.

In a quick move, Jake snaked an arm around the front of her waist and shoved her behind him. Half-way across the room, he heard the buzzing of voices and swung around. A faint light streamed across the room from the screen of the television. Cursing himself for leaving his service revolver in the car, he wound his way through the rooms.

Her heart racing, Leigh sagged against the door for support. Up until this moment, she'd thought Jake was being too cautious—almost paranoid—about Seaton. But he'd been in her home. In disbelief, she stared again at the half-eaten apple, left like a calling card.

Fifteen minutes after Jake's phone call, a mob of uniformed men were tramping around the woods behind her house. From the edge of a sofa cushion, Leigh eavesdropped on Hamil, who was conferring with his men on her front porch.

"Ms. McCall." Leigh jumped at the sound of Hamil's deep voice. "Did you own any guns?"

"Never," she said in a sharp tone that swung attention on her.

"Could you tell us if anything is missing?"

Her head throbbed at the back of her skull, as if a vise were squeezing it. "I'll have to look around."

Al took an uneasy step forward. "Probably she should start in the kitchen," he suggested.

Hamil gave him a semblance of a smile. "That would be a good idea. Chances are he took supplies so he could hide out again."

Jake trailed her into the kitchen. He took an angry drag on a cigarette. Seaton was laughing at them. He'd chosen her house deliberately, to prove she was within his reach.

Holding open a cabinet door, Leigh fixed a stare on cans for a long moment and tried to concentrate. Thinking suddenly seemed like an alien act. "Do you remember if I had beans?"

"Three cans."

"There's none here. A bottle of water is gone. A bag of nuts." Leigh faced him with an uncertain smile.

"This is impossible. I don't remember what I had here. Do you?"

Stepping away, he flung open the refrigerator door. "The fruit is missing. Juice. *My* can of beer."

Ridiculously, a laugh tickled her throat. Though it stemmed from nervousness, she wanted to hug him at that moment for trying to calm her down. "Keep looking. I'll check the bathroom."

As she stood before the linen closet, Hamil sidled close. "A sleeping bag is missing, too," she said. "I kept it rolled up and stored on the bottom."

Unsteady, Leigh stayed in the bathroom, gulped down several aspirin then rubbed the back of her neck. In the mirror, she saw Jake standing behind her.

He'd already searched his mind for words to ease her worry. He'd thought of nothing. As her eyes met his in the glass, he rested his hands on her shoulders. Seaton wouldn't hurt her. No one would again. "Lie down for a while."

Her head throbbing, she wanted to do that, but a proper upbringing insisted she go into the kitchen. Against Jake's protests, she stayed and brewed coffee, and when Kathleen arrived within the hour, offering sympathy, together they assembled sandwiches and set up a table in Leigh's dining room for the men involved in the search.

Outside, media from the last checkpoint swarmed in on her front lawn. Cameras poised while reporters with mikes pursued anyone who came out of the house.

Tired of the noise, the houseful of people, Leigh dragged herself to the bedroom.

Jake left her alone. He examined the cut screen door and splintered wood at the doorjamb. Beacons of light played across the woods in an eerie succession as men searched with flashlights.

Feet from him, Hamil barked orders over his two-way radio in response to a garbled message from one of his men in the woods.

Worry marring his face, Leigh's uncle shouldered open the screen door and held out a coffee cup to Jake in a token of friendship. "I thought you could use this." As Jake took the cup, Matt McCall scowled at the dark woods. "My niece is ready to disown everyone in her family except Kathleen, I think." As if it took effort, he met Jake's eyes. "About what happened years ago—"

"I didn't think you were a part of it."

"I knew. So I guess I'm just as guilty. I knew your father was innocent."

Jake gave a brief laugh. "I wouldn't say that description ever really suited him. But he didn't set the fire."

"I should have come forward. I should have said something but..." He paused and shrugged one shoulder. "Hal and Abby. They were my family. To go against them ... I—I couldn't do it."

Revenge never had been Jake's plan. Only truth had mattered. Noting the deep lines in the man's face, Jake gripped Matt's shoulder. "Let's get something to eat." Jake made it halfway across the kitchen with him.

Downing water, Al raised a halting hand. "I'm heading out to Janzer's now."

The announcement tempted Jake to go, too. Sitting still and waiting went against his natural instincts, but he hadn't been there for Leigh once before when she'd needed him. He damn well would be this time. "You know where to look?"

"Oh, sure," Al said, drying his mouth with the back of his hand.

"Be careful. Don't play hero."

"I ain't crazy. If I see anything, I'll be back."

Tired, Jake stepped over several snoring men sprawled on the carpet in Leigh's living room. Quietly he entered her bedroom. For a moment, he simply stood and watched her draw steady, even breaths. Because he hadn't taken care of her before, he needed to now.

He slipped into the bathroom and held a washcloth under the spigot. Maybe it was because she was such a strong, independent woman that he needed to pamper her a little.

A weak smile curled the corners of Leigh's lips as an unexpected coolness suddenly bathed her forehead. Cautiously, in anticipation of the throbbing behind her eyes, she opened one eye and touched the cool washcloth.

Sitting on the edge of the bed, Jake studied her face for pain. "How's the headache?"

"Better. I'm just tired."

"Then sleep for a while."

Leigh reached up to caress his jaw. "You haven't slept all night, either. Lie down with me."

Dark eyes filled with soft tenderness beckoned him. As she turned over, he obeyed the command of her hands on his back urging him down. This was what he'd come in for, he realized as he drew her into the crook of his arm. He'd been yearning to hold her, to give—to receive.

He knew he'd slept. The question was, for how long? Holding her against him, he rested his cheek against the crown of her head and listened to her quiet breathing, to the absence of sound outside.

The rain had stopped, making the manhunt easier. Where was Seaton? In the woods? Close enough to see her? He shifted slightly with thoughts of getting up.

Beside him, the phone rang. Involuntarily he jerked. Cursing his own jittery reaction, he shot an arm out and fumbled in the dark room to stop its shrill ring before it awakened her. "Yeah," he mumbled low, still groggy from sleep.

"It's me, Al."

Jake opened and closed his eyes several times. Beside him, Leigh stirred and uttered a soft moan.

"I checked that mining shed. I think he's there."

Jake was already easing his arm from under her neck. "Where are you?"

"At the gas station on the corner."

It took a moment to register what he'd said.

"It seemed better to telephone than come rapping on the door. Want to go with me?"

Sitting on the edge of the mattress, he raked a hand through tousled hair. "I'll be down in a minute."

Beside him, Leigh pushed to her elbows and peered at him. "Where are you going?"

"They might have Seaton cornered." Jake dragged himself to a stand, then hauled up his Levi's. "I'm going."

Sitting up, Leigh snapped away her drowsiness with one thought. The fear shadowing her might soon be over.

"You don't have to get up," he said between breaths as he yanked on a boot.

Leigh stood and pulled a T-shirt over her head, then tugged on her jeans. "I know," she answered, wiggling into her sneakers. "But I'll walk you out."

When they got to the living room, Al was already there, pacing like an expectant father. "We'd better hurry," he said, sounding more than anxious.

Leigh caught the edge of nervousness in his voice. "Afraid you'll miss the capture?"

"Could happen." He kept moving back and forth a few steps as if to hurry Jake. "I tailed Emmy Phillips. She went into the wood shack about three this morning."

His head bent, Jake slipped on his shoulder holster. "Who's out there?"

"Uh, no one." Al shook his head. "Everyone's out in the woods. Eddie and a couple of highway patrol guys catching some Zs are the only ones here besides you and me."

"Did you call Hamil?"

Al sort of came to full attention. "Right away. But they figure it's gonna take them an hour or better to get back here, and he said that you should, uh—"

"Come on."

Standing at the door, Leigh grabbed his arm. "Wait a minute." A bucket of ice water thrown at her couldn't have jarred her awake quicker. "I thought you were just going out there to help. You aren't. You're going out there to get him, aren't you?" Leigh felt her heart catch, felt a trace of perspiration trickling down the small of her back. "Why? This isn't your business."

Al's eyes darted from her to Jake. "I'll wait outside for you."

Leigh stifled panic to keep her voice calm. "Why are you doing this? Because you want to be some hero in this town?"

Without touching her, he sensed her pulling away. "No, because it is my job. Leigh, I'm a cop. You never stop being one."

What she'd dreaded most was upon her again. Foolishly she'd dodged the inevitable. She couldn't accept his life. No matter how much she loved him, she couldn't live with the day-in and day-out danger he'd face. "I know," she answered quietly. Against her will, her voice trembled. "But I forgot." For a heartbeat, she considered begging him to give it all up. How could she? Such selfishness would haunt them.

"When I come back..." The shake of her head stopped him.

She turned away, refusing to meet his eyes. Above all else, she didn't want to bury another person she loved. "Don't come back here, Jake."

He swung her around, disbelief in his eyes. "What are you talking about?"

"I made a mistake."

"You said—"

She cut him off. "I can't. I can't handle this." She shook her head. "Always wondering if this time will be the last time I see you, I talk to you."

He needed a moment to catch his breath. "You don't mean this."

"I do." As he touched her shoulder, she stiffened. The heartache was starting. She couldn't escape it, but it would be more devastating if she gave in to love, if she began a life with him. She never wanted to raise children alone, see the suffering on their faces because their daddy was a cop, because he'd sacrificed everything to do his duty. It wasn't the life she wanted for herself or any more children she might have. "I told you how I felt." She drew a painful breath. "I'm sorry. I should have never let any of this happen. I can't go through it again."

Frustration churned inside him. He wished for the right words. He was a pragmatic man who believed in facts, in what was visible before him. He couldn't think of any way to penetrate her imaginary terror. A helplessness to stop what was happening drifted over him. "I've made love with you. All the denials in the world don't mean a damn to me. I know what I felt, what you were feeling."

It would have been easy to lean into him, not to think about what ifs, but she knew better. The hurt now couldn't equal what she might feel later if she lost him.

As she started to step away, he grabbed her arm. "What we feel for each other matters more than anything else."

She wished that were true, but fear was such a part of her that she couldn't think.

Desperation swept over him. He was determined not to let her go, afraid that he might never touch her again. "How can you do this to us?" he whispered challengingly.

She fought the knot in her throat. "It won't work." Even as she said the words, she swayed. Surrender was a breath away. She struggled, as she'd struggled since he'd come back. With one phone call, reality had slammed back at her, reminding her that love didn't banish all obstacles.

"Tell me what you want, what you really want."

You. She ached for him, for the love given and received so freely ten years ago. For the innocence that blinded them then to everything but that love.

"Do you want me to give up what I do?"

As if he'd struck her, Leigh drew back. "I can't ask you to do that."

"What do you want from me?"

"There is no answer." Her heart twisting, she saw his hurt, but couldn't stop herself. "Nothing you say, no amount of love, will take away the uncertainty that goes hand-in-hand with the risks. There are risks. You're taking one right now, and you don't have to. I can't live this way. I've gone through this before. I can't go through it again." Leigh yanked her arm free from his grip. "You go and do what you have to do. But don't come back. Please," she pleaded softly. "Don't come back."

Nothing else she might say could have sliced him open so effectively. The urge to shake her, crawl to her, rushed him. "You're fooling yourself. You don't stop loving someone because you want to." He snatched up his Windbreaker. "I know. For the past ten years, I tried."

Chapter Fourteen

Her back to him again, she waited until she heard the slam of the car door. She couldn't say why she did, but she rushed to the window. She reached it in time to see Jake driving away. Fears and doubts consumed her. What if he and Al walked into an ambush? Seaton had guns, ammunition and no desire to go back to jail.

Oh, God, she didn't want to feel this. She didn't want to weep or care or love. She didn't want to be hurting again, but she was. And she'd hurt him. She'd seen the look in his eyes. It haunted her while she finished dressing.

Quickly she hopped in her car, but she sat as if paralyzed. She knew where he'd gone. If she followed . . . She blocked the thought, not letting it completely form, not allowing memories of the days and nights they'd shared to stir misgivings about her decision.

Within minutes, she reached town. The usual stillness of daybreak was shattered by the droning of a helicopter. Visually she followed it, waiting for it to turn in the direction of Janzer's property. Instead, it flew north toward the woods.

Keep busy. Don't think. With no more than a nod to her uncle, she hurried in and began to wait on customers. Fear was with her, tightening her throat, squeezing her stomach as she circled the restaurant and refilled coffee cups, as she thought of Jake in the woods.

For a second, she could almost hear gunshots. A hand on the closest chair, Leigh forced herself forward and fought the horror in her mind. She couldn't keep doing this. Concentrate on something, anything.

At the counter, Lester was in good form for so early in the morning. "The mayor said they're closing in on Seaton."

Tilting his head slightly, as if he had trouble hearing, Clyde leaned toward him with interest. "When did you hear that?"

"Last night."

Leigh moved away, letting Lester go on with his version. No one had known Seaton's hiding place until right before dawn this morning.

Weary, she produced a semblance of a smile for a customer. It slipped away as she swung around. Through the wall of windows, she saw a deputy's car across the street and Eddie rushing into the sheriff's office.

Only a second passed. Leigh flew to the door and raced across the street. Why would Eddie have come back to town? When she'd left the house, he'd been one of the few men available. They'd need him. He wouldn't have left unless—

She hit the sidewalk at the same moment Eddie charged out of the office. "Why are you here?" Leigh snagged his arm. "Did something happen?"

"Nothing yet." Looking down, he wiped a hand across the dust on the box cradled in his other arm. "I came to get these."

Dumbly Leigh stared at the small carton.

"Tear gas. From the storage room," he explained.

That news didn't help. "Before you left, were Hamil and his men there yet?"

Eddie skirted around her to jump into his cruiser. "No." He started up the engine. "I hope they are by now."

Leigh was trying to understand. "You didn't go in after him?"

"Jake told us to wait until daybreak," he called back. "He..." Whatever he planned to say went unfinished. Distracted, he stared at the mayor's car pulling away from the curb. "That's just what we need. Tebner looking on. If we blow this, Al and I will both be unemployed."

Leigh stared after him with a look of disbelief. More was at stake than their jobs.

* * *

Even before Jake had arrived on Janzer's property, he'd weighed the situation. Darkness had mantled the woods and the door of the shed, which was choked by shrubs. Acting foolish had never been his style. He stationed men in strategic positions around the shed.

Sitting beside him in the Jeep, Al was nervous and impatient. "How long do you think it'll take before the rest of them arrive?"

Jake glanced at the clock on his dashboard. "They'll be here soon."

"I saw movement, Jake."

Al's words straightened him in his seat. Eyes fixed on the shed, Jake set his mug on the dashboard. "Let's move in."

Al's audible breath announced his anxiousness.

As far as Jake was concerned, this show belonged to Al and Eddie. They could be heroes if they wanted to take advantage of the opportunity. Jake figured that decision should be theirs. "Do you want to wait?"

"No." Al set his jaw with determination. "If you say so, we'll go."

It was the response Jake had expected. He gave Al a quick grin and they pushed open their car doors. From behind them, Eddie scurried forward to them with a box. Together, the three men crouched low and stalked closer to the shack.

When push came to shove, Jake couldn't let go of this work. He'd fallen into the slot of a dedicated cop. Get the bad guy. He believed in good over evil. It was a principle he lived by, one he'd never be able to give up without losing a sense of himself. It wasn't a choice, he reflected as he and Al moved one way and Eddie circled around the back. Without his work, Jake knew he'd lose. But, damn, would he really be alive if Leigh wasn't with him?

Leigh lumbered back into the diner. Neither she nor Kathleen were managing a convincing act. Noticing the shadows under her sister's eyes, she halted Kathleen with a touch on her arm. "Something happened?"

Shrugging, Kathleen tried to move away.

Leigh danced around her to block her path. "Kathleen?"

"Everything's wrong."

Leigh didn't ask for more of an explanation. She ushered Kathleen insistently into their uncle's office. "What's wrong?"

Side by side, they perched on the edge of the desk. "Jim lied." Tears brimmed her eyes. "He kept saying he planned to settle down here. This morning he made the big announcement. He wants to go with Dale."

Confused, Leigh frowned. "Go where?"

"Indy." Kathleen swept a hand out. "Wherever."

"Start from the beginning," Leigh said, too muddled to make sense of the tidbits of information.

"He told me last night that Dale offered him a job as head mechanic with his pit crew." Puzzlement clouded her eyes. "I don't understand. I always seem to pick men who want more adventure in their lives." Head bent, she toyed with her receipt book. "Do you think some women pick the wrong kind deliberately? Do you think I do?"

Leigh heard traces of self-blame slipping into her sister's voice. "Slow down. *You* don't do anything wrong."

"I must."

"Oh, Kath, don't do this to yourself." Leigh didn't think she was getting the whole story. "What did Jim say about the two of you?"

"Oh, he wants me to go with him." She twisted the book in her hands. "I've been through this kind of life before. There's never any security."

Leigh knew her sister was reliving the past with another man. She'd moved with him constantly because of his job and had hated it. "It might be different with Jim," she offered as encouragement.

"For me, alone, I might try it. But what about the kids? They deserve more than being hauled all over the country. They love it here. They have friends. This is home to them."

Leigh thought a reminder was necessary. "They'd make a home wherever you take them."

Kathleen managed a soft, mirthless laugh. "You're right. They're good kids."

"So why are you *really* refusing to go with him? If you love him—"

Kathleen spoke more calmly. "Okay, say we go with him. And one day he leaves, just like Larry did. He packs a bag, says he wants more than I'm giving him, whatever that is, and the kids and I are stranded in some place far from here." Sadness edged her voice. "I've gone through that once. I don't want it again."

Leigh heard her own words echoed in her sister's. Hadn't she said the same thing to Jake? "This time could be different."

"It doesn't feel different. I couldn't make Larry happy." A wry smile curled her lips. "Not enough for forever."

"You aren't responsible for what someone else feels."

"But they don't love me enough. I never meet one who loves me enough." She slid a hand over Leigh's. "Look at you and Jake. Ten years. And he still loves you just as intensely as he did before. Anyone can see that. And you still love him, don't you?"

"I never stopped loving him," she admitted sadly.

Kathleen shifted slightly to face her. "Oh, Leigh, I've been rambling and..." She looked toward the door as if visualizing the diner. "Why isn't he with you?"

"He's with Al and Eddie. They're going to get Seaton."

"You mean, all of them—the FBI and...?"

"Only a few of them."

Kathleen appeared uneasy. "Don't you think he's a good cop?"

"I'm sure he is." Leigh eased off the desk and crossed to the office window. "But even good cops get killed." The sound of more voices from the diner alerted her that it was crowding with customers. "We should go out."

Kathleen moved beside her. "Not yet. We have a few more minutes." She squinted, as if trying to view

Leigh more clearly. "You're pulling away from him because he's a cop?"

"I have already. It's over. I told him so this morning."

Kathleen sighed heavily. "Oh, we are a pair. I have at least two reasons that are close to my heart for backing away from Jim. But you don't."

"I have a good one."

"So you've stopped seeing him and now what? Mark? You don't love him," her sister said with certainty.

"Okay," Leigh snapped, angry more at herself than Kathleen. "Call me a coward. Do you remember how Mom worried about Dad? Do you remember the night you and I waited for word about him and Ken? Do you remember what you and I went through when we learned they were shot? I do. I can't live with that worry."

"What difference does it make what you *say*. It's what you feel that matters. And whether you broke off with him or not, you're still worrying."

Leigh stared in astonishment at her.

"I'm making sense, aren't I?" Kathleen asked, smiling for the first time that morning.

Leigh didn't want to admit it. "No, you aren't. If you were, you'd realize that there's a bigger chance that Jake might be hurt than there is that Jim will do what Larry did. So what if Jim wants to go somewhere else? It shouldn't matter. It doesn't change who he is, change him from the man you fell in love with."

"I'm putting conditions on love."

"Yes, you are. You say you don't want to go through that again. That you don't want to live the life he leads. But you're running from what might happen...." Her voice trailed off.

So was she. "Oh, God." Leigh drew a hard breath. Suppose he lived a nice long life. Suppose nothing ever happened to him. Not all cops got hurt. Why hadn't she remembered that? More importantly, why had she blinded herself with what ifs? Because it took courage to love again, really love someone.

She'd been such a fool. Because of her own cowardliness, she was giving up all the happiness she could have with him.

Kathleen's face brightened. "You're going to him?"

Leigh gave her a quick hug. "You bet." She dashed to the door, but paused to look back at her sister. "And you?"

The uncertainty and sadness had settled back on Kathleen's face. "I'm scared."

Scared. Leigh was scared, too. Scared of what she'd nearly lost again because of her own fear. Nothing mattered but what she felt for Jake. She'd lost the man she'd loved before. Not again.

Jake nudged a handcuffed and coughing Seaton out the door of the shed and through the shrubs then nodded to Al to take him the rest of the way. His man in custody, Al swaggered a bit as he led Seaton toward Hamil and his men.

Her head bent, tears streaking her face, Emmy Phillips moved at Eddie's command.

Jake shoved through the brush to his Jeep. There was no reason to stay anymore. He'd sold the property. He'd learned the truth about his father, about why he'd never felt comfortable in Pineview. There was nothing left to be gained.

"Quite a coup. Quite a coup that our boys got him." Tebner beamed, doing a double step to catch up with Jake. "I must say that's going to do a lot of good for this town."

Jake recalled Al's steady actions before they got Seaton into custody. "They're good deputies."

"Al told me they had a good leader."

Jake kept walking.

"We need a sheriff."

"Well, you have two good men to choose from."

"Yes, I do, but they don't have the experience for the job. We need someone who knows how to handle any problem that comes our way. The town council's been discussing that for the past week," he rambled on. "This business with Seaton made us aware we have to hire a sheriff. Because we didn't have one, we were in the dark about this business." A little winded, he grabbed Jake's arm to slow his stride. "We'd like you for the job."

Jake stopped abruptly. "What?"

"We had several meetings and we'd like you to be our sheriff. We know you're settled in the city, but we need you here."

Sheriff? He couldn't believe they'd offered him the job. He rolled the idea around in his mind. Pineview's sheriff would face minor problems: a rancher's son who thought back roads were trial runs for a speedway, vandals who enjoyed painting mustaches on the faces of billboard advertisements leading into town, and town council members who'd pressure for more security every time a misdemeanor was committed.

Tebner shifted his weight from one foot to the other. "We hope you'll accept."

"The town council approved?" Jake said with incredulity.

"It was unanimous."

Jake let those words sink in. *Unanimous.* Everyone.

"Now, to be honest, the pay isn't like you get in the big city. And the pace is slower. But we have a lot of fringe benefits here." He laughed at his own joke. "If I remember right, you cut a lot of my history classes to go fishing."

Jake returned a slim smile.

"You could take a couple of days to think the offer over, but this is your town." He patted Jake's shoulder in an affectionate, fatherly manner. "We'd really like someone who knows the area and understands the people. One of our own."

One of our own.

In his whole life, he'd never been more stunned by something someone had said. Jake walked slowly toward his car, deep in thought. Even if he accepted, he wouldn't have the one person in his life who meant everything to him. No matter where he worked, she wouldn't accept the danger or the risks.

He glanced around him before sliding behind the steering wheel. One last look, he mused. He'd come home, was finally accepted, yet he felt alone. A crowd could surround him, here or in the city, but he'd still feel as if a piece of himself was missing. It would be worse this time, he knew, even as he tried to shove the feelings aside. They weren't kids anymore. Man and woman. They'd loved. They'd shared some of the most difficult moments with each other. They'd comforted each other over the loss of a child. They were bonded in a way they hadn't been years ago. And yet, for her, it wasn't enough.

He started the engine and eased the Jeep past a throng of reporters. He'd go back to Leigh's and get his bag while she was at the diner. Within an hour, he'd be gone.

Chaos greeted Leigh on the dirt road leading toward Janzer's property. Braking before her, highway patrol cruisers threw plumes of dust in the air. Parked in helter-skelter fashion, they blocked the path of media vehicles racing down the road.

Leigh scooted out of her car and worked her way through the crowd. Her courage crumbling, she prayed, but kept elbowing her way through. She had to believe he was all right. There would be other times like this, but the waiting, no matter how long, was worth even a second with him. She couldn't let fear control her. There was too much to lose.

A band of uniforms formed a barricade, stopping hungry reporters. Around her, voices buzzed, raising with excitement. The push of the media, the flash of cameras, followed. The undercurrent of excitement made her edge forward. "Do you know what's happening?"

"They got Seaton."

Reporters trapped Hamil and barraged him with questions.

Not seeing Jake, Leigh searched for a familiar face and latched on to the mayor's. "Tell me what happened."

"Seaton's in custody." He grinned broadly, as if he'd captured him single-handedly.

Again, Leigh visually circled the men standing around. "No one was hurt?"

"Nope. Got him without a gun fired. Actually, Jake did. Al, too," he added. "They threw tear gas in, and he never put up a fight."

"Have you seen Jake?" she asked, scanning the crowd once more.

"I saw him get in his Jeep."

"He's gone?" The words held more of a meaning than he'd guess. Gone. Again. Only this time, she'd sent him away. "Thank you," Leigh said, whipping around.

"Whoa." He seized her arm. "You could be helpful."

Leigh stared at him dumbfoundedly.

"The town council offered Jake the sheriff's job. I told him it was unanimous."

Her head spun with the news. "My aunt—she...?"

"Astounding, isn't it? When we discussed it before, she was adamantly against the idea. Then she said yes." He held his hands out. "Just like that."

A warmth of happiness flowed through her for Jake. She knew how much that vote of confidence must have meant to him. She knew, too, that she'd fallen in love all over again, this time with the man who'd gone into law enforcement, who cared about people, who wanted to protect them, who pushed past his own bitter memories from his youth to help the very people who'd made him feel so alone. If he hadn't been like that all along, he wouldn't have been so devastated in his youth at feeling like an outcast.

"See if you can persuade him to take the job. We know he's got an important one in the city, but—"

Suddenly impatient, Leigh glanced at her wrist-watch. "When you asked him, what did he say?"

"He didn't give me an answer. I told him he could have a few days."

She ran for her car, doubting she had even a few hours.

The five-minute drive to her house *seemed* like a matter of hours. What if he'd left already? What would she do then? She'd follow him, she decided.

Her heart pounding, she raced down the street. As she made the final turn, she sighed with relief at the sight of his Jeep still parked in front of her house.

She wasn't too late.

With no idea what she'd say, she rushed from her car toward the steps. On the second one from the bottom, she nearly stumbled as he came out with a carryall bag in his hand.

Dark and intense, his eyes carried a message of hurt. Her back straight, she raised her chin as if ready for a punch. She wanted to step into his arms, but so much needed to be said first. "You're going back to the city?" Silent, he kept studying her, making her nervous. "I heard that you got an offer for another job, too."

Jake tightened his grip on the handle of the canvas bag. He wanted to pull her close, but he couldn't hold her, couldn't self-inflict the pain he knew he'd feel when he had to let her go. "You talked to Tebner?"

"He mentioned the offer." Suddenly worried she might have hurt him too much, she kept up the small talk for a little longer. "My aunt agreed. That's a miracle."

"Unexpected." He'd hoped to avoid this kind of moment. "I'm almost out of here. I thought I'd be gone before you came home," he said, descending another step.

She had so little time now. "There was no problem this morning? With Seaton, I mean."

He held his arms out as if for inspection. "Not even a nick."

"I was told no shots were fired."

"There wasn't any need to."

"The sign of a good lawman." At the puzzlement in his eyes, she took a hard breath and plunged forward. "They'd really like you to consider their offer."

She was close enough to reach. Jake shoved a hand in his pocket to keep from touching her. "It might be awkward."

"Awkward?"

"With you here, too."

"Would you have taken it if I wasn't?"

The question seemed ridiculous to him. "There's no reason for me to be here if you aren't."

"Oh, Jake." Leigh hurried up the step. She reached a hand toward his face and crumbled a little inside when he drew back, shying from her touch. "I'd like you to take the job here," she said quickly. "But if you don't want to, then I would go anywhere with you."

With a thud, he dropped his bag to the step. "Anywhere with me?"

The wind blew at her back, as if nudging her closer. "Anywhere," she whispered, feeling anxiety sweep out of her as his hands touched her waist.

"Leigh, this doesn't make sense."

"Of course it does." Coiling her arms around his neck, she stared at his mouth, doubting she'd ever stop wanting the taste of his lips. "I love you. You love me and—"

"That wasn't enough before."

A surge of panic rushed up at the difficulty of the moment. "When you came back here, you had to deal with old feelings. I had the same problem. No matter how much I'm afraid, even when I'm not with you, I'll still worry about you. Does that make sense?"

His lips curved in a slow smile. "Yeah."

"When I realized that, I also woke up to something else. I was scared. I've loved and lost so much. But if I didn't stop being afraid, if I wasn't willing to take some chances, I was going to lose again. I don't want to live my life without you."

He couldn't help it; he wanted more. "What about marrying me? Would you want to walk around this town with the last name of Ryker?"

She curled a hand around the back of his neck. "I should have had it years ago." Holding him close, she knew some fear would always shadow her, but she couldn't let past pain or the alarm aroused by her imagination rob them of happiness. There were no guarantees he wouldn't be hurt, but then there were none that he would be. They could grow old together. Only a fool would turn her back on a chance at years with the man she loved.

Gently he brushed her hair back from her face. "Let's go inside."

They got as far as the sofa.

With her beneath him, desire stirred. Lightly he grazed the soft curve from her waist to her hip. For a moment, he said nothing as he realized how close he'd come to never knowing the feel of her again. "There's nothing I want more than to make love to you at this moment."

Leigh leaned back into the cushions and tugged him closer. "What's stopping you?"

On an elbow, he held his weight from her. "I know the fear you've had. I wish I could take it out of your life, but I can't. Life doesn't carry any guarantees."

"I know," she murmured, kissing the corner of his lips.

"But I'll give you the same one I made ten years ago. I'll love you forever."

Snug beneath him, she smiled. "I don't need anything else." Suddenly impatient, she framed his face with her hands, her mouth seeking his. She kissed him, love for him filling her. A love that wouldn't allow for anymore goodbyes.

Skimming his back, she released a husky laugh. "What I said isn't really true."

Jake's brows drew together. He couldn't imagine any other problem.

"I still need to know where we're going to be."

Staring at smiling dark eyes, he brushed his mouth across hers. He had a choice he'd never expected. He could go back, but memories would always lure him to this town. He had a chance for a new beginning as a respected member of the community. And he'd have her. "Tebner reminded me that I always liked to fish."

She laughed again, happy about his decision, pleased that he'd finally learned there was a place in this town where he belonged. "Whatever you say, Sheriff."

Leading with his shoulder, he rolled her with him to the carpet. Letting the moment seep over him, he buried his face in her hair. "How about that," he said close to her ear. "Jake Ryker, sheriff of Pineview."

No hesitation burdened her. "They made a smart decision."

Head bent, he toyed with the buttons on her blouse. "Think so?"

"Know so," she assured him. "But the town council members aren't the ones to worry about."

In fascination, he watched her lips curve in a half-amused smile. "Who is?"

"Me." She curled an arm around his neck. "You're lucky you didn't get shot, or I'd have killed you."

His head went back with a laugh. "Sometimes you make no sense."

Her eyes became serious. "Until now, I haven't." Before his mouth captured hers, she murmured, "Or I'd have known we were meant for each other." Eyes closing, she parted her lips for his. "Always."

* * * * *

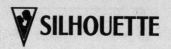 **SILHOUETTE**

SPECIAL EDITION

COMING NEXT MONTH

HUSBAND: SOME ASSEMBLY REQUIRED
Marie Ferrarella

That Special Woman!

Shawna Saunders knew that fleeting seduction—not lasting love—was Murphy Pendleton's stock in trade and he saw her as a challenge. Would he just get bored one day and walk away?

A RING AND A PROMISE
Andrea Edwards

This Time, Forever

Jake MacNeill didn't know why he'd felt the need to visit Chicago, but he knew he wasn't going home without Kate Mallory! Surely it couldn't have anything to do with the love their ancestors had shared?

THE BEST BRIDE
Susan Mallery

Hometown Heartbreakers

Sheriff Travis Haynes was Glenwood's leading lady-killer, but he'd certainly rescued Elizabeth Abbott and her daughter when they'd needed him. Travis could shatter an already bruised heart, but he was awfully tempting…

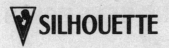
SILHOUETTE

SPECIAL EDITION

COMING NEXT MONTH

THE ADVENTURER
Diana Whitney

The Blackthorn Brotherhood

Devon Monroe and Jessica Newcomb both had tragic secrets,
and the power to heal the other's pain...if only they could
trust their hearts.

A BED OF ROSES
Elyn Day

Michael Gordon healed damaged bones and sprained muscles
but he was having trouble fixing his own broken heart. Would
taking a chance on Dana, his angry and frightened new client,
lead to a sweet bed of roses?

THAT SPECIAL SUNDAY
Maggi Charles

Russell Brandon Parkhurst had lied to Paula. He'd been less
than honest about his huge fortune, his rocky youth and even
his name. Why should she believe he loved her?

COMING NEXT MONTH FROM

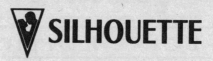 SILHOUETTE

Intrigue

Danger, deception and desire—
new from Silhouette...

ONLY SKIN DEEP Rebecca York
WHO IS JANE WILLIAMS? M.J. Rodgers
IN THEIR FOOTSTEPS Tess Gerritsen
WITHIN THE LAW Laraine McDaniel

Desire

Provocative, sensual love stories for the
woman of today

A NUISANCE Lass Small
BRANIGAN'S BREAK Leslie Davis Guccione
CHANCE AT A LIFETIME Anne Marie Winston
INTERRUPTED HONEYMOON Modean Moon
MIRACLE BABY Shawna Delacorte
PERIL IN PARADISE Diana Mars

Sensation

A thrilling mix of passion, adventure
and drama

ONE LAST CHANCE Justine Davis
A SOLDIER'S HEART Kathleen Korbel
MISTRESS OF MAGIC Heather Graham Pozzessere
TWO AGAINST THE WORLD Mary Anne Wilson

SPRING FLOWER COMPETITION

How would you like a years supply of Silhouette Special Editions ABSOLUTELY FREE? Well, you can win them all! All you have to do is complete the word puzzle below and send it in to us by 31st November 1995. The first 5 correct entries picked out of the bag after that date will win a years supply of Silhouette Special Editions (*six books every month - worth over £150*). What could be easier?

COWSLIP	L	L	E	B	E	U	L	B	Q
BLUEBELL	P	R	I	M	R	O	S	E	A
PRIMROSE	I	D	O	D	Y	U	I	P	R
DAFFODIL	L	O	X	G	O	R	S	E	Y
ANEMONE	S	T	H	R	I	F	T	M	S
DAISY	W	P	I	L	U	T	F	K	I
GORSE	O	E	N	O	M	E	N	A	A
TULIP	C	H	O	N	E	S	T	Y	D
HONESTY									
THRIFT									

PLEASE TURN OVER FOR DETAILS OF HOW TO ENTER

HOW TO ENTER

Hidden in the grid are various British flowers that bloom in the Spring. You'll find the list next to the word puzzle overleaf and they can be read backwards, forwards, up, down, or diagonally. When you find a word, circle it or put a line through it.

After you have completed your word search, don't forget to fill in your name and address in the space provided and pop this page in an envelope (you don't need a stamp) and post it today. Hurry - competition ends 31st November 1995.

Silhouette Spring Flower Competition,
FREEPOST,
P.O. Box 344,
Croydon,
Surrey. CR9 9EL

Are you a Reader Service Subscriber?   Yes ❑   No ❑

Ms/Mrs/Miss/Mr _____

Address _____

_____

_____ Postcode _____

One application per household.

You may be mailed with other offers from other reputable companies as a result of this application. If you would prefer not to receive such offers, please tick box. ❑

COMP195